The Tune of Murder

~

B.A.L. McMillan

This is a work of fiction. Names, characters, businesses, places, events and incidents are either the products of the author's imagination or used fictitiously. Any resemblance to actual persons, living or dead, or actual events is entirely coincidental.

Formatting and cover design by Stephanie Flint

ISBN-13: 978-0-9895034-0-2

Published by LiquidAmber

Henderson, Nevada

Dedication

To lovers of music, musicians, and mystery.

Contents

~1~

Guest

LUKE MICHAELS COULD SEE THE SIDEBAR OF THE BED FRAME inches above him, and thought it too thin and polished to be any part of a cross, and yet it was, distinctly that, in his mind and heart. He would have touched it except that he could not lift his arms. One of his hands was palm-down on his abdomen and he recalled with great peace that he was injured. He wasn't dying, though, only falling toward sleep, something very pleasant to him. And music was rushing through him. He heard it in his head and felt it in his body, and less so, though warm, against his hands. He hummed it with his entire fading self. The cross of music, music and the cross, love eternal, love. Love. Music. Sweet blessed love music. Blessed music.

* * *

Dizzy with nausea, Johnny gulped the night air and scrambled with his arms laden toward the old taxi. He laid the things down on the street, unlocked the trunk—how stupid he had been to leave it locked when he needed to throw things in hurriedly. Of course, he hadn't known he'd be sick, too. He hated nausea worse than anything. Worse than pain. Pain was nothing. He didn't retch, though. He wasn't leaving any of his bodily fluids around. He heard a dog somewhere. A high yelping one, which meant a little dog. He swooned. He wished he had a place to go, where someone would take care of him. He wasn't meant for this kind of thing. But he had done it, by God. He put the stolen items in the trunk, lowered the lid and pushed down. The latch didn't catch completely, but he left it that way. The lid wouldn't open; it just wasn't shut. That was right where he lived his life—halfway in everything.

* * *

Monday afternoon, as the pawn shop owner headed toward the back rooms, Johnny suspected he was now in deep trouble. The man was likely going to call the police. But the recorders and microphones were already behind and under the counter somewhere, and his own name already on the yellow record. So he held his ground with a little bit of hope. The owner came back, not smiling, eyes hard and knowing, and said, "I don't have enough right now to pay you. My wife's bringing some more cash over. Only be a few minutes."

"I'll just take my stuff and bring it back later."

The owner shook his head. Johnny started for the door, but there they came, already out of the patrol car, adjusting belts, seriously studying the glass windows and him through them. Deputies. Johnny sighed. Personally, he liked law officers. He would like to be one. Fat chance. In the midst of the next few moments, he'd be the lowlife. He'd sold himself short. Nothing new about that.

Johnny felt like he was being transported to a foreign country. Everything was alien. They brought him in through something called a port, but it was simply an open garage. Still, he felt they had landed and everyone else was comfortable. They were going to abandon him. He had to go into a building, a little glass lobby, and look into a machine that took pictures of his irises. A few feet inside the next door, he stood by a chair while the officers talked around him. It was steel, with straps that went over legs and arms and one around the head or neck. Maybe an old electric chair—but why have it in the first room of a jail? He answered every question he could. When they told him he could phone someone, he asked, "Can I do it later?"

"You bet. Good idea."

Two of the officers accompanied him down a very short passage to the left, a metal bench lining the wall. A metal rail recessed beneath the bench was scratched up, as if people had been chained to it, which he supposed was the case. The hall ended at a square room with sloping floors and a drain. He had to disrobe, shower, and then they searched his body, a process he had heard about, but still found humiliating, though they were professional and quick. They gave him an orange jumpsuit to put on and orange rubber slippers. Then they led him again to the entrance area, but by a high, round, plastic control center where a woman officer sat before an instrument panel. Part of it resembled a soundboard. Three microphones, too. The men stopped partway down the hall, in front of a door on their left, between huge glass windows. A sign taped on the wall nearby read POD A. He could see inside, though it was sort of muted, as if the glass had been shaded. He assumed it was one-way glass. He would be on display for whoever stood outside. Now the big room was empty except for two orange tables with orange benches around them, and a television high up on a wall. He wanted to ask if orange everything was ordered by regulation, but he couldn't speak easily yet. His throat wouldn't work right, he was pretty sure. They took him inside, and up metal steps to his left. At the top were four doors, though there might have been more since the upstairs was at odd angles like a maze.

"You're the only guest today," the officer said. "It'd be a rare day in hell if we had more than one maximum security guest at a time." He sounded friendly enough, not sarcastic.

One officer stayed at the top of the stairs which was just outside the room, and the other went inside with Johnny. A big concrete block that was part of the inner wall held a thin mattress. No pillow. No blanket. A steel commode with no lid was about three feet from the block bed, in a corner, and a few feet from that on the other wall a metal slab jutted out like a desk, only there was no chair. He was feeling a little panicky.

They had his cigarettes and the little wad of money from his pockets. He read the name tag of the officer with him. "Officer Jakowski, could I have my cigarettes?"

"Not in here. If we're not shorthanded, you can go downstairs four times a day for meals and snacks and to have a smoke. That's at 5:00, 12:00, 5:00, and 9:00."

"What about now? Could I have a cigarette now?"

The officer studied him, head cocked like he really was weighing the matter. He shrugged. "Why not?"

Downstairs, they let him have two cigarettes. Both of the officers stood up, arms crossed, legs apart, watching something on the silent television.

Johnny didn't see a television remote anywhere. They probably decided what he could hear and when. He didn't care about television anyway.

He realized he couldn't see through those huge windows into the hallway. He could be seen from out there, though. He was on display. He'd had a baby alligator once, kept it in an aquarium. His parents got rid of it.

"I'd like a soda," he ventured.

"You're in early enough for supper, and you'll probably get on the commissary list for tonight. It's your cash they'll use for junk food, and believe me, the stuff costs. It's one of our best sources of revenue. We're leading the country in innovative ways to finance our own department."

They took him upstairs and left him. This might be the rest of his life. All steel and concrete and plastic and rubber and craving and loneliness.

If his dad would just come up those stairs and unlock the door and say, "Okay, Johnny. We're going to work this out. It's not the end of the world."

But it was.

Crabwalker and Handyman

MRS. DUNBAR, A DIMINUTIVE, WHITE-HAIRED WOMAN, SAT ON the back steps of her Victorian house, which was a small-scale copy of one just west of it. She was staring raptly, ostensibly into space, but actually she watched gossamer webs float like slivers of light, visible, then not, then visible again—baby spiders on their way to their future. She wished she could see up close how they wrought their magic, jetting silk into the air and, once airborne, continuing to jet silk strands as needed. Maybe they knew which breeze they wanted and could select a destination, even a continent, or choose to stay airborne all their lives. They didn't have to eat for months, and probably could catch organisms without landing. There would, though, also be predators. Always predators, gaping beaks, darting tongues, sharp fangs—driving hunger. Not evil. Nature was harsh and violent. So it was in the whole world. Man and womankind were themselves part of the same grand natural system, predators and prey. But there was beauty, too! Some of these shimmering little creatures would alight, and spin a future, make prisms in gardens and in sunlight and shadow. Survive. And if fortunate, enjoy what they were meant to enjoy. They, too, would kill to eat. What else could they do?

Spiderlings.

The ringing phone broke into her thoughts, and she scurried inside, her hunchbacked body twisting around the kitchen table, into the living room. Breathless, she said hello and was surprised to hear an operator announcing a collect call from Johnny Rowland. He was her great-nephew and had never in his life called her. She feared the worst—something had happened to his parents.

"Yes, I'll accept the charges," she said.

"Aunt Lettie?" came a cautious voice. "This is Johnny."

"What's wrong?"

"I'm in jail. Don't get real upset, though. I didn't do what they say I did. They say I murdered someone, but that's not true."

She sat down in the nearby rocker. "Of course you didn't." She looked out the window to the side yard, where a brewer's blackbird strutted, head stretching upward. "Can you tell me why they think you did?"

She listened intently, and took quick notes on a small pad of yellow paper. When the call ended, she ate a dry saltine cracker to protect her stomach and took two aspirins with a tiny paper cupful of water—her remedy for most ailments. Then she went outside, toward the alley, to see if her neighbor's vehicles were all there, indicating he was home.

To her right, her shadow elongated, more hunchbacked even than she, just inches ahead of her and growing, as if it might outpace her.

"Crabwalker," she muttered with disdain.

Galway's truck was gone. The other two vehicles glowed in the murky light. She hadn't seen him drive either of these, but he kept them clean.

She stood under the remnant of eave, feeling imprisoned by old bones and heart. She wanted to *do* something vigorously. Rescue Johnny.

A thief? That would be enough to grieve over. But murderer? Don't let it be!

Johnny was at least nineteen, but that was very young. And she thought of him as younger still, as the nine-year-old who had sobbed and said, "I won't say I'm sorry because I'm not sorry." Such fortitude, to choose a spanking rather than violate his own principles. "I'm not sorry." Oh, honey, she thought, shaking her head again to make the sad feeling go away. Oh, Johnny boy.

A fat, bow-legged dog, obviously part basset hound, nosed down the alley and paused to look at her. She nodded but didn't speak—if she encouraged friendliness, she could be knocked off her feet. Bassets were a boisterous, showy breed, and would claim an entire sofa if allowed. Once they felt ownership, they defended it. This one seemed to consider the cane with a rolling, lazy eye, and trotted on. She would never have raised the cane unless she was forced to do so, and bassets, though they had a powerful bayhoo, weren't vicious dogs, didn't attack unless they were loosed on a hunt.

She liked dogs, cats, birds, turtles, toads, katydids, beetles. Children. Creation.

* * *

On a gray-shingled, pitched roof about five miles away, Galway Evans had briefly stopped working in order to hear completely Garcia and Grisman's "Down in the Valley." It was an old song, and unbelievably sweet as they did it. Sentimental and touching. At this moment, that song was his favorite. Absolutely. He couldn't bear not to hear it. He sat down on his skinny haunches. Along the southern horizon gray and black clouds were billowing up, the bottoms flat, like a bunch of bullies threatening but staying just behind the line. Silent lightning flared behind the clouds.

If you don't love me, love whom you please,
Throw your arms round me, give my heart ease.

Some versions didn't include that verse. Another version changed one word, said "Put your arms round me" instead. He liked that best, he supposed, since it was more subdued, the kind of embrace someone might give who didn't love the man. "Throw" might mean false exuberance, a really ugly trait.

The song over, he clicked off the radio. He had to finish. He had cleaned all the horizontal gutters, surprised at the number of treelings sprouting from just rotten leaves and a modicum of dirt. He had hated to scrape them to be thrust into garbage bags with other gunk, because transplanting might be possible. But not necessary. No. He had hosed out four downspouts, too, but then— then he had encountered this one, apparently packed solid. There was a good word for that, which he wouldn't say. He had cleaned out the bottom section as far as his trusty coat hanger would reach, and now knelt by the top, hooking out clumps of matted leaves, twigs, berries, feathers, walnuts—though there was no walnut tree in this yard—straw, and crushed, white, miniature blossoms.

"How's it going?" came from below. The lady of the house.

"Almost done. This one's clogged."

She watched him for a few seconds. "I'd hate to have this . . . debris on the ground when it rains. It'll spread out and you'll never get it cleaned up."

"I'll take care of it. Don't worry."

His hands were dirt-streaked, nicked and scraped, with a couple spots a little bloody.

One rule about lightning was you could be struck by it even before you could hear the thunder.

He clambered down the ladder, tugged the readied hose up with him and thrust the nozzle as far down the spout as he could, twisting it open to full force. In seconds, the water shot-sprayed out and riveted up the sides, stinging his face and neck and splattering his clothing. The sludge stank, musty and sour. Some was on his lips. He kept them clamped shut, held the hose right where it was, and the splattering lessened. He felt the gurgle as if it were a live thing, and then the absence of it as the blockage broke up, flushed down and out. He guided the hose deeper, released it, unrolled his shirt sleeve and used it to wipe his face.

"Damn well did that," he muttered.

When he came to the door with the carefully trimmed down and signed bill, he could see her inside, standing before a television set. He couldn't hear the announcement, but he recognized the format as a news flash. He said "Miss" rather softly, but she jerked around, coming toward him with "Are you finished? Good. I . . . I heard the most disturbing news." She fingered the hook latch. He couldn't tell if she was lifting or lowering it. "A young man I know was murdered. A boy from our church."

"I'm sorry to hear it." He didn't know exactly how to handle this, so he just raised the invoice.

She pushed the screen door out and took the bill. "Is this all?" she said. "I'm surprised, but very glad. Did you clean up the mess?"

"I did, and put the bags by your trash pickup. I'll haul them away if you prefer."

"No. I'd rather the regulars dispose of it. I'll be right back."

She shut the main door, which he understood. She was scared and he was a stranger. Still, he felt a tinge of resentment.

The door opened, and she slipped the check out for him. "I'll pass your name on," she said. "It's so good to find a reasonable handyman."

"I thank you for your business, and I'll be glad to come back if you need anything. I was thinking you might want a storm door. You'd feel more secure."

"Thank you." She closed the door.

"Idiot," he said, headed for his truck. He had frightened her with innuendo. Not deliberately. He had the finesse of a buzz saw.

* * *

When Galway drove away, the home owner ventured out to walk around her house and see that the man had truly cleaned up. What if he had been a killer and she had foolishly left her door open all the time he was there? Of course he wasn't a killer. He wouldn't have parked his truck for everyone to see, and left his handwriting and . . . He could have opened a window, though, or broken a lock, or unscrewed a porch light, planning to come back! In fact, he could have already come back, and be waiting on her right now. She whipped inside and held her cell phone while she checked out all the doors and windows. When everything proved clear and safe, she had a piece of marble cake, and thought of having clean gutters before the storm, which was so accidentally timely. She managed fairly well. The handyman seemed a decent sort, but it was very odd that he was in that line of business. Men who got on roofs or climbed trees needed some muscles. Round muscles were best. Short, round-muscled men were usually agile and strong. They could even work on the steel girders of high rises. This guy, this—she looked at the receipt—Galway Evans, he was a string-bean, more like a character in a ghost book or scary movie, someone who might wear robes and grow a low whispery beard, or someone who could fiddle a wild, foreign tune, or leap from building to building, or catch the talon of a giant bird and be flown away to safety. He had done the job, though.

She remembered the newscast and her earlier nervousness

returned in part. Luke Michaels. The young man was dead. Murdered. He had a very lovely voice. Had had. It was a shame. The old phrase *Only the good die young* came to her. She didn't know anything about Luke Michaels, but she doubted the phrase was true. She tried to think of evil people, and came up with many names, but none had died young. She tried to name their victims and couldn't. She felt thwarted. It was a bad subject for a widow.

* * *

On the way home, beneath a gradually darkening sky, Galway listened to one verse of Prine's "Souvenirs," then switched to a pop station. Something thrummed his truck, and since he didn't see a semi anywhere that could have caused it, he assumed it was thunder, and snapped off the radio. Lightning did hit cars. He removed his watch and put it in the cup carrier.

Galway's strange little neighbor, Mrs. Dunbar, was waiting for him, standing still as a gnome under the west eave of his make-do garage. It was really an ancient building, maybe from the late 1800s, a blacksmith's shop. The wood was so hard it wouldn't take a nail. Next to it were stables, the same hardy stock, useless except that he valued what they had been. He could get all his vehicles in the shop, but if push came to shove, he could park each in one of the stables. Horses of a different breed, buddy. He enjoyed the whole business, the house, the grounds. The quirky neighbor.

"It took my breath away," Mrs. Dunbar said, when they were in his kitchen, and he could see that it truly had. She wouldn't sit down, but stood with her back to the counter, left hand on her cane and the right lightly pressed over her heart. It was more a delicate stance than an alarming one, totally natural, and yet he saw the stress behind it.

"He said," she continued, "that he did steal, but they've charged him with murder, and he did not do that. I believe him. I don't think he's capable of it—oh, maybe accidentally, but not on purpose. And he wouldn't lie. I just don't believe he'd lie."

"I understand. We'll do something. Just sit down here for a few minutes, will you?"

She was shaking her head before he pulled the chair back for her. He raised his hands in capitulation.

"I'm too nervous to sit down," she said. "I would shake from it, and that scares me. It's not pretty either."

She smiled, so he did, too. She was all right.

"He wants me to help him, and you're the only help I know."

"I've never handled that kind of legal problem, Mrs. Dunbar, but I know some very good attorneys. I'll get in touch with one of them right now."

"Can't you represent Johnny yourself?"

He almost said "yes" because he was inordinately fond of her already, for no reason except that she had won him over the first day he met her, and because she seemed to be extraordinarily familiar to him, like a relative from some off branch that he recognized without knowing why. And "yes" because practicing law was still his most familiar endeavor, and withholding that assistance seemed selfish. Fortunately, he wasn't the right person for this situation. "It would be a disservice to both of you. I haven't had much experience with this kind of case. And experience matters, believe me."

She looked more than disappointed. An energy had left her.

"Let me make a phone call for you. Just a minute." He tapped the chair back, not pushing her, just reminding.

In the hallway, he heard the sound of cupboard doors being opened in the kitchen. Up to her own ways. He went on to a room that had probably been the smoking room and was now his office, with a huge desk before a Gothic bay window—the bench part long enough for a person of normal height to lie looking at the sky—a leather, high-backed chair, a good stereo set and albums shelved on one wall, and books on all the other available wall space, and some stacked on the floor. He plopped down, opened the bottom right-hand drawer and stared at the carton of cigarettes while he called an old friend, and recent colleague. Andy Fielding, attorney at law. Successful, honest, meant for the job.

Andy accepted. "I'll see him this afternoon and I'll call you later tonight or in the morning. Why don't you work on the case with me?"

The answer should be no. But in the kitchen was that gnome, somewhat in pain. "Yes," he said to Andy. "Just let me assist."

"Do you want to come along for the first visit?"

"No. Two people always make a third seem the outsider. I'll talk with him in the morning."

"Keep me posted. By the way, how are you doing?"

"Pretty good. I cleaned gutters today. It was a bit harrowing. The clouds were moving in and I felt like a lightning rod."

"Given your height, you were. Seriously, it's good you're doing something you like. You've had a tough time."

"It's going as it goes. I don't want to talk about it."

"Then we won't. I'm glad to have you working with me for whatever reason."

* * *

Andy Fielding spent the next few minutes thinking of Galway Evans, who had changed immeasurably, shrinking into himself and looking out as if his soul had burned. He used to laugh often, a catchy sound recognizable anywhere. A happy, soft-hearted guy who chain smoked and kept music playing in his office—some station that played music from around the world.

* * *

Mrs. Dunbar had put lunch on the table, two tuna fish sandwiches, each halved, gherkins, potato chips, and a glass of iced water.

"Marry me," he said, and saw her suppress a smile.

"I didn't have to thrust my problem on you so quickly," she said. "You're a working man. And anyone can fix tuna."

"Timing is everything. Yours is perfect. About your nephew— an attorney friend of mine, Andrew Fielding, will see Johnny this afternoon. He'll check the crime reports and anything else he can. He'll call me, and I'll call you."

She nodded. "Fine. Thank you."

He unfolded the paper napkin she had put to the left of his plate. "Are you going to join me?"

"I'm not hungry."

"You really should eat more, Mrs. Dunbar. You could gain ten pounds or more without it showing."

"I hope you don't think that was a compliment. I'm healthy. I don't comment on your physical appearance. It's extreme, you know. Between the two of us, you look the more frail. I'm just bent."

He chuckled. "Truce," he said. He ate half a sandwich and a few potato chips. "I knew about the murder before you told me. The woman I was working for heard it on the news. She said Michaels was from her church."

"Who was that?"

"Mrs. James Wren."

She perked up. "Myra Wren. She sang in the choir with Luke. The news must have startled her. Even a natural death can rattle you. This . . ." She shuddered. "It's different when it's someone you know." She looked aside a moment, added, "and when the murderer may be someone you know, too."

Galway was anxious to leave now, but she had prepared the food for him, and he didn't want to diminish her gesture by not eating it all. He took another bite and another, rushing enough that she did notice, but said nothing. "I'd like to find out where this Michaels lived and go over there. Maybe I can beat the rain." He considered asking her if she wanted to ride along, but he didn't want her getting more excited or more depressed.

She screwed the lid on the gherkins, reached for a paper towel. "I'll clean this up."

"Just leave it." He could tell that didn't take. "At least don't do any extra work."

She nodded, but he saw the quick glances around his kitchen.

"I'd be uncomfortable with you cleaning it better than I do," he said. He took one of his cards from his pocket, scooted it across the table. "My cell phone is on there, if something comes up."

She was wiping off the gherkin jar. "You wouldn't want an old woman in the truck anyhow. It would make you look suspicious immediately."

Had she wanted an invitation to ride along? Even if so, she was correct that she would make him look suspicious—more than he already did.

"Next time," he said.

* * *

With Galway gone, his kitchen back in order, Letitia Dunbar headed to her own house, feeling useless and slow. She had embarrassed herself, being a supplicant, and then wanting to go along. No matter how quick a mind was, the body could drag it down. She thought of Johnny, unfortunate young man. He had been the cutest kid, with that red hair and big eyes, and a petulant will to irritate his mother and father. "I'll tell your parents about the situation," she had told him earlier. "I'll tell them as gently as I can. But I need to do so in person, so it'll be a couple of hours. Just try to get along where you are. Don't get flippant."

At the bathroom sink, Mrs. Dunbar dampened her palms and pressed them against her up-pinned hair. It was thin now, but still curled. If it didn't, her scalp would show, as she had seen happen to older women. They'd sit in church fancied up, presenting the best selves they could, and the light through stained glass would make their hair a faint, delicate mist over a round scalp. Hats probably became popular for that very reason. And buns, too. The lower, thicker hair grown long so it could be pinned high to mask a balding crown. Changes could catch a person ill-prepared emotionally. Age crept up on you. Life took quick turns and set you on a path you hadn't anticipated.

Who was that wily old woman in the mirror, with pale blue eyes and eyebrows so white they showed up only at their thickest point? "You, old gal," she said. "You."

The rain had begun without her hearing it, and was a pleasant surprise. It seemed to quicken her and the world. She was off, engaged with every moment, with the slickness of the back steps and grass, with the little puddles holding miniature black shadows, with the shiny streets reflecting traffic lights, and cars whishing by, as if they whispered something.

* * *

Zeena, Johnny's mother, magpied a welcome as if the words were meant to discourage and block any incoming subject. Her black eyes were highly accented today, with dark eye-shadow extending the outer edges like butterfly wings, the brows above equally dark and arched. It was a witch look to Mrs. Dunbar, especially given Zeena's attire, long black skirt with an over-tier of black lace, a black, gauzy shirt with high collar, buttoned down the back. Her hair, usually down or piled high, was in a sleek roll around her lovely face, a look from the 1940s that was coming back. Red lipstick delineated the shape of her mouth but had worn off in the center, probably from nervous pressing together of her lips.

"It's been too long," Zeena repeated. "Really. We should see more of you, and just get together for whatever reason. I'm as guilty as anyone, because time goes by and I have so many projects. I plan to do this and that, and then Peter changes my plans or Johnny does." She hovered over that thought a moment. "Which is usually a needless aggravation. Now Peter's on the back patio. I'll get him, but he'll have to clean up. He's been working in dirt for hours. He takes a day off every now and then to catch up on yard work or read. He says he should have been either wealthy or a gardener."

They were in the dining room. A long rosewood table with eight matching chairs dominated the center of the room and other heavy pieces lined the walls. There was little space around it, disallowing any guest of generous proportions. Zeena had paused by the sideboard, running her tiny fingers inside her waistband as if it were too tight. "I've been experimenting with homeopathic therapy, especially through teas and candles. Some have purifying qualities, some sedative, curative. You know."

Mrs. Dunbar knew very little about such things, but she wasn't disinterested unless it edged into the occult. She was healthily wary—not superstitious, not judgmental, she hoped, but wary. Now, she noticed a rather thick, almost palpable aroma in the room. She could taste it and considered the source. Zeena's current arsenal covered the top of the sideboard, bathed in the soft light of a lamp at its end: baggies of herbs, each labeled and tied with a gold cord, like party gifts; several books aligned along the carved oak back, testifying to the powers of the collection. All of them together were adding a bit of scent to the already crowded room, like invisible minions, maids of Zeena's order.

"I've tried herb gardens," Mrs. Dunbar said, "but I'm never sure the plants are clean. My mother used to clean vegetables with a wee bit of bleach water. She rinsed them forever. I won't use bleach, but I wonder what's still on a leaf. Is it truly possible to clean away every trace of snail slime—snail track, I mean? Snail track. It can cause a horrible disease. I know some dirt is healthy and being too fastidious can ruin a life, but some natural elements are naturally disgusting."

Head tilted slightly to one side, Zeena was studying her coolly. "That surprises me, coming from you. I thought you worked in the yard a lot."

"I do. I just don't eat anything if other creatures are partaking of it before I do."

"What about produce from the store?"

"It's three or four times removed from the questionable diner."

Zeena laughed, despite herself. Mrs. Dunbar was grateful to have the lighter mood. The room seemed larger, and the air clearer.

"Well, don't worry about my herbs," Zeena said. "I keep snails out of my garden. There's a soil that cuts them to pieces as they crawl over it. There are other poisons, too. You can kill slugs by putting out shallow dishes of beer. They're drawn to it and they drown. An old method was soot. Oh, Letitia. You should see your face. All a person needs to do most of the time is to clip off any part of a plant that's diseased or too soiled. Pay attention to the garden, take care of it. It doesn't take too much time, but you will have to stay on top of blights and insects if you want to have a healthy product."

"It's not the kind of effort I can stay with, Zeena. At least I don't want to try."

"Many people don't want to and couldn't if they did. Many also confuse folk remedies with magic, and then don't trust the herb. I think maybe you do that, especially about these herbs." She indicated the bags on the sideboard. "There's an art to growing and storing herbs, especially if they're not just for cooking. These aren't drugs, if that's what you think. I won't have anything to do with drugs. But they do have true medicinal properties. They're beneficial."

Mrs. Dunbar wanted to say that most plants and minerals had medicinal properties, yet were poisonous, too. But she understood Zeena's attempt. "You're becoming an herbalist. Good for you. I mean that. Everyone should pursue an interest. It's a major joy in life."

"I do enjoy it. Thanks."

There was a shy, childlike quality to Zeena's appreciative smile. Mrs. Dunbar felt sympathy for her, but she had a task and readied herself to speak to Zeena the mother. "I came by to give you a message from Johnny."

Zeena's light smile was gone, replaced by a weak impassivity. "Okay," she said.

"He called me because he didn't want to worry you, and he's fine, physically. He's not hurt or anything."

"But he's in trouble."

"Temporarily. It's a mistake."

"I'll get Peter."

"Zeena."

Zeena was striding away, the hems of her layered skirt undulating around her feet like dark waves. She headed not for the patio, but for the stairs. She muttered "damn, damn, damn" as she ran up them, a slender shot of fear.

"He needs some help," Mrs. Dunbar said, heavy with her own mishandling of this. She should have waited, have talked with Peter and Zeena together, or perhaps with Peter alone.

Mrs. Dunbar went in search of Johnny's father and found him sitting on the concrete floor of his roofed patio, a series of flat cardboard boxes before him, each filled with a pile of grass runners and clinging black soil.

"Hey, Lettie," he said. "Look at this Augustine grass. It likes shade, so it ought to do fine here. We usually grow more mold than we do grass."

In a few short minutes, she told him about Johnny. His face softened, sagged. Without the smile, he looked much like his father, with prominent jowls like an old-time, eastern seaboard judge. He carefully settled the handheld clump of runners in the nearest box, cleared the strands from tangling with another clump, and brushed his hands on his jeans. "He couldn't call me, could he?" He shook his head, sighed. "I've never hurt him. I don't even yell at him. I don't like angry voices either. But why would he call you instead of me? I guess he thought you'd go easy on him no matter what. I might want to, but . . . He doesn't even want to see us, huh?"

"He said he didn't, but why else did he phone? He's afraid to ask and probably afraid to face you. I was afraid, too."

"Yeah. I know. Bearing bad news. Or, in the case of Johnny, being bad news, I guess." He looked up, quickly. "To his mother. Not to me."

"Not to her either, I imagine. She just exercises what control she has. You'll have to decide if you want to see him, Peter. He admits he was stealing, but insists he didn't kill anyone. I don't think he's lying about that."

"I hope not. He doesn't usually lie. He just does exactly what he wants and bears the consequences. He's going from bad to worse. I'm sorry you had to get involved, Lettie, especially when it's ugly like this."

"We're all in the same family. I'm automatically involved, and want to be."

Lightning cracked, and they both looked at the steady, mild rain.

"Aggravating Missouri weather," Peter said. "I thought I'd have the whole afternoon to putter. Maybe we should get in the house proper. Last year a guy in the Bootheel got struck when he opened his door to check on the storm. It's funny in a way. I mean, he just wanted to know how it was doing and he learned." He chuckled. "I know it's sad, not funny. I'm sorry. Really." He still smiled, but was trying to straighten his expression. "Really. I'm sorry."

"You needn't be. It is ironic. An outsider can see the quirk of fate and laugh at that alone, not at the tragic part of it. Anyhow, Peter, I'm going on home."

"Stay here. You don't come by often enough. We could wait till the storm passes on."

"It's just a hovering one. It'll spend itself soon."

"We could go see Johnny together. It would be easier on all of us."

Mrs. Dunbar shook her head no.

"Just stay awhile."

Upstairs was a brooding, fearful Zeena. Mrs. Dunbar wanted to go up there, rap on the door, and say *stop wallowing in self-pity and self-righteousness and get yourself down the stairs and to your son. And your husband. You flea-brained ninnie.* She bit slightly her lower lip, right side. Who was she to fault anyone? Zeena had her own obstacles. Everyone did.

Johnny was a sweetheart.

"I'm sorry, Peter. You and Zeena don't need me monitoring your troubles."

Mrs. Dunbar, driving by squinting through the rain-swept windshield, wondered if she herself were the pathetic creature here. She had never even had a child, though she had wanted to have many of them—seven. She had names chosen, paired up, and in the early years of her marriage had silently offered them to fate, a dream of family: Jeremiah, Joshua, James, Joseph, Jude, Jonathan, Jesse. She had tried to insert Judith and Josephine, but the shameful truth was she hadn't wanted daughters, only sons. What kind of woman was she, to spurn her own gender like that? Selfish person.

The punishment was no children at all.

She would have liked a son similar to her neighbor, that tall, rangy Galway Evans, dear boy, who had inexplicably befriended her and brought some kind of charm into her lonely old age. What would she do if he moved away?

* * *

Zeena heard Letitia leave, and shuddered with the release of tension. She felt wilted, spent, unable to stand up to the demands even of verbal exchange, much less the meeting of accusative or sympathetic eyes. Other people's emotions played her like a harp, and Letitia, Aunt Lettie, was so absolute in nature, so always right. It was unbearable but also laudable and left Zeena with nothing but inadequacies, even if Zeena was right! In the right! Now she whipped around and strode to Johnny's room. She took a packet of matches from one of the pockets of her practical—and beautiful, she thought, really nice and beautiful—skirt. She had placed candles in each window and, though rain still fell and thunder rolled over the house like a long growl, she opened the windows a few inches, lighting a candle in each. *Be safe baby*, she intoned very low, only a murmur under that growl. *Be safe in this circle. I think you in this circle with me.*

* * *

Luke Michaels' address was in a residential area just outside the city limits. Yellow tape strung between short plastic rods cordoned off the building and a few feet of the yard. It was a small, boxy house, the inside layout fairly evident from the shape and the windows. There wasn't enough room for much creative space inside. It rested on concrete corner posts and probably, though they weren't visible, other support columns beneath it. Raised houses were common in this part of the country, where heavy rains caused drainage problems. Also common was the inexpensive lattice, white in this case, sealing the underside. The building's front faced east, the door in the center of a deep porch and flanked by two standard windows. Three south windows were street-side, one of them smaller and higher, perhaps leading into a bathroom or utility room. Outside the taped area a flimsy carport shaded a flat, grassless spot. Galway meandered that way, checked the corrugated sheets from beneath. Nails protruded here and there, dangerous for a tall person, especially a clumsy one. A cheap kit and poorly assembled.

He strolled beside the tape, examining ground and house. After all, he was a citizen and not crossing the boundary. The lattice work was uneven along the backside. No gaps, but two panels appeared to overlap. Again, there were three windows, one likely above a kitchen sink, one in a bedroom, and a smaller one between them. Beneath it, smudges marked the white siding. On the ground below were two slump blocks. One had fallen over, but apparently the two had been stacked to aid the burglar's entry through the window. The fellow hadn't been too adept—a good thief left no sign of the personal, unless, of course, it was a deliberate miscue.

Mrs. Dunbar's Johnny had probably done everything but sign his name.

Galway rounded the far corner of the staked yard. He wanted to get inside. It lured him, the feeling that he'd find something for sure, something no one else noticed. He nibbled his lip, considering just boldly trying the front door. Why not?

"You're pretty interested in that house."

Startled, Galway turned. The speaker was an elderly gentleman about ten feet away, at the edge of the adjoining, deep green and well-seamed turf lawn. He had been in the heat a while, or wasn't too well. His face and neck bore a ragged flush. His eyes, poor guy, were red and rheumy.

"I'm interested in all of them," Galway responded, "since I'm looking for work. But I did hear that someone was murdered in this one. I was giving it the once-over. Partly morbid curiosity, maybe, but I'm also wondering about the condition of the property."

"You a clean-up crew?"

"Never that, I hope."

"I heard there's good money in it. I saw that in a movie. If you have a strong stomach."

"I don't, not that kind of strong. I'm in another line of work. Do you know what happened to him?"

"I heard he was stabbed. I know they found him on Sunday. They took his body out then. I watched the whole thing. Saw it on the news, too. The woman that lives there," he pointed at a pink residence across the street, "called the sheriff. She saw the guy that did it."

Galway extended his hand. "I'm Galway Evans. I'm looking for odd jobs, nothing too big since I don't have much equipment yet."

"I've got a little job. It's a rotten fence post in the back yard. The ground slopes there, so rainwater pools around the post. The moisture's rotted the bottom half. You want to give me an estimate for a new post?"

"Glad to."

"I used to do these things myself," the man said, leading the way, "but my wife gets upset."

"That's not good."

"I'm ninety, but I could still handle it."

"You don't look ninety."

"My wife knows my age. No fooling women, you know. Let me revise that. No fooling *wives.* I don't know much about fooling other women." He laughed, a blustery, congested sound.

While the old gent identified the problem, Galway surveyed the victim's house from this angle.

"So what do you think?"

Galway shifted his full attention. The bottom portion of the post was soft, almost spongy. "It might be difficult to match the style. I don't know what it's called, but it's different. Very nice. Would you like to save it? I might be able to clean out the rot and rebuild the bottom."

"Repairing it is no good. We have enough falling apart. I'd rather have something new and sturdy. As for matching the other posts, that doesn't matter so much back here. Nobody's going to care much about the fence style but me and my wife anyhow. Something similar would do well enough. What would it cost me?"

Galway gave a moderate estimate.

"That's more than reasonable."

"As I said, I'm trying to build up a practice."

"I think you want to be building a business or service. No one wants a handyman to *practice.*" Again came the laugh-cough. He gave Galway a quick look, spoke more soberly. "Cheap prices is a good start, but good work is the best way. Don't undersell yourself or people'll think you're either not any good or up to no good."

"I do good work. It may take me longer than some people, but I'll do it right and I don't charge by the hour. This," he indicated the post, "I could do this week."

"You just go at it, then. Good thing I spotted you."

"Did the guy next door rent? The owner might want some minor repairs done."

"He lives out of state. I don't know who does his maintenance."

"That carport's likely to fall down."

"The kid put it up by himself, as far as I could see. Not exactly a lovely addition to the neighborhood."

"What kind of car did he have?"

"You sure you're not interested in more than work? You're asking a lot of questions."

"I guess I am. It's a habit, and one I should probably curtail. But there's a carport and no car. The guy is dead. It's odd."

"Yeah. It is, isn't it? I can't answer your question. People came and went. Sometimes they parked in the street, sometimes in the yard—that was before the carport. He didn't beautify the place, but he was a decent enough neighbor. He didn't cause me any trouble. The music was a little loud now and then, but not too bad. Of course, my hearing's older than the rest of me."

Rain had reached this neighborhood, the smell of wet grass coming before Galway felt any drops. He urged the man, Mr. Welker, to go in, reassured him that he'd be here on Thursday, if not before, and then loped across the street. He glanced back to see Mr. Welker still outside. Maybe his home life was what turned him florid. Though Galway intended truly to look for more jobs on this street, he headed for the pink house.

The woman answering his knock was about forty, red-haired, with severely crippled hands. The knuckles were huge and the index fingertips turned sharply inward. She seemed glad to have company, even invited him in, though she left the door open. At her feet, a red-orange Pomeranian yipped and spun and darted constant warnings at Galway. She listened to his short business introduction, accepted his card, but had no work at present. He squatted down, his hand offered low and slow to the now fiercely growling dog. It snuffed a few seconds, sniffed his fingers, allowed its snout touched.

"Mr. Welker told me a little about the victim across the street. He said you saw someone over there."

"Are you a reporter?"

He shook his head. "No. Truly a handyman. But a friend of mine goes to the same church as the victim did."

"I didn't know he went to church. I don't, so . . . Yes, I did see someone. She," the woman indicated the pet, "had been acting up for quite a while, and I finally looked out the front window. A man was getting in his car. Instead of driving off, he backed up quite a ways, and stopped. It seemed odd, but a lot of young people gathered over there now and then. I thought maybe a party was happening. On Sunday, though, I saw the police cars, all the commotion. I went over there. Then I told them about the car the night before."

"So you didn't report anything Saturday night?"

"No."

Galway stood up. The Pomeranian's nature flared again, snap, yip, yap, yap, yip and spit. A lion's mane attacking on its own.

"No one would break in here," Galway said. "You have a good watchdog."

"I do." She smiled down at the creature. "You're a darling, aren't you?" She looked back at Galway. "I can't pet her like I used to, and I think she misses it. It makes her edgy."

Galway lined up a couple more jobs and was drenched when he finally got in his truck. He didn't mind. He left the window down until a couple lightning cracks warned him to roll it up. As he drove home, he thought about the dog longing to be petted and the mistress longing to pet.

He parked in his make-do garage. The wood was ancient, almost petrified, with deep grooves and gouges from weather and time, black as pitch. Old, old. He patted the top of the BMW as he walked past it, and then ran in his long-legged way toward Mrs. Dunbar's house instead of his own. She would want to know what he had learned and he wanted to tell it.

When he had first seen her, she had a project underway and was unaware that he watched. She was kneeling on a towel by her back steps. Beside her, a child's red wagon held a bag of quick-mix cement, rags, and a few hand tools. In front of her was a galvanized bucket, shiny new. She scooped a few handfuls of cement into the bucket, picked up a trickling garden hose, added water to the mixture, and stirred it with a trowel. A scowl on her features indicated her dissatisfaction. She added more cement, and stirred the mixture with her hand. Then she applied a handful to the corner of the steps and tried to smooth it into place. It didn't cling.

"Damn," she muttered, and slapped the loose pieces away. That's when she saw Galway. "Excuse me," she said. "But the recipe they give doesn't work."

He helped her. He hadn't mixed cement either, and she was right about the "recipe." But they eventually patched the concrete base of her wooden steps. The wagon and supplies she stored in a small utility shed on the west side of her house. "I can move almost anything with that wagon," she said. "It's helpful when I buy too many groceries or the bag person packs too much in one sack. They burst easily."

"If I weren't here," he asked, "how would you get the bag of cement out?"

"I would dump it," she said, "by tipping the wagon."

Galway set the bag nearby, so the wagon would be free for the next chore.

Later that day, he heard his back screen door rattling, and found Mrs. Dunbar there, with the wagon behind her. Whatever it held was covered with a white cloth.

"Are you a vegetarian," she asked.

"No ma'am."

"Good."

She had brought roast, potatoes, gravy, green beans, and banana pudding.

He understood. She believed in paying her way.

Now he wasn't surprised when she responded to his report with "I'd like to see inside that house myself."

"It might not be so good for you. I'll see it for the both of us."

"Then take notes, please. Draw it for me."

"I can't draw."

"Just stick figures. Like writing with signs."

"I can do that."

"I'm wondering if Johnny's the one who called the sheriff," she said.

"Why do you think that? Did he say something?"

"No. But I think if he knew about the murder somehow, his conscience might have made him call. He'd think he could keep the things he stole, but even the score by notifying the sheriff about a murder that he didn't do."

"Doing a good deed to wipe out a bad one."

"Maybe not wipe it out, but make it paler."

There was something enigmatic about her, as if she had a secret and was on the verge of telling him. Maybe all old women—elderly women—had that quality. She was the first one he'd ever exchanged more than a few words with.

* * *

At home, Galway thumbed the letter W on his cell phone, scrolled down to Walter Hildy, an old school pal, red-haired and alabaster skinned, presently the duly elected coroner, at the end of his first term. So far, it hadn't interfered much with Walter's life, which was mostly fishing in still, loggy water. He liked catfish.

"Walter, buddy," Galway said, "would you let me see the photos of the Michaels' crime scene, or, better yet, get me in the house?"

"I think that's against the rules."

"Don't check. Just answer me."

Walter thought how nice it was to have Galway on the other end of the phone. He felt friendship linking them again and he wanted to make it permanent. "Good to hear from you. I'll work it out."

Galway sighed. "Thank you."

"I'll get the thing set up."

Galway felt a bit guilty for asking a favor but not for bending rules. People came first and most regulations were relative. Almost everything was relative. Is honesty the best policy? Or is kindness? Is it better to have loved and lost or never to have loved at all?

His throat constricted.

Better not to grieve or at least to get the grief over with quickly.

He opened the bottom drawer of his desk. He wanted a cigarette. If he had one, he'd have three in less than an hour, maybe more than that the next hour. He wanted one so bad he could eat it. He closed the drawer with his foot. He could wait this minute. He put on an album of Cajun waltzes, turned the sound up, and left the room. The music reached him in the kitchen, where he opened a can of tomato juice and sipped it, the lively voices beginning to elevate his spirits. He couldn't do a waltz to save his life, though he knew the pattern. One, two, three, one, two, three. He tried it, stopped, finished the tomato juice, crushed the little can, dropped it in the trash, and went out to sit on the porch.

* * *

Johnny ate dinner in his pod alone. He went to the opaque glass and, cupping his hands around his eyes, leaned close to it. An officer on the other side smiled at him, and seemed to give a little laugh. Johnny withdrew, sat at the table. In a few minutes the officer came in and lighted Johnny's cigarette. When Johnny crushed the remaining butt into the macaroni and cheese, the officer said, "That's it for now. I have a report to write up."

Then an attorney came, called, Johnny understood, by a Mr. Evans for Johnny's aunt, a Mrs. Dunbar. This was home ground! Johnny was close enough to family to feel affiliated with the world outside and to feel trust for this attorney. He liked him anyhow. He considered the pointed face the face of an angel. He didn't want to be a groveler, so he held back, tried to be restrained and straight-forward, though there were details he couldn't give, wouldn't give, ever. He liked being really close to someone who wasn't in uniform, and able to reach out and touch the person if he wanted. They hadn't let him bring a cigarette in and he could tell by looking at the attorney that the man didn't smoke. He was thin like a runner, with thick, jet black hair, very neatly combed, though it was so very thick. His hands were tiny, but he wrote quickly. The pen just flicked, spitting curls of ink that flattened into words.

"So how do you think you got blood on your shoes?" Mr. Fielding asked.

"Like I told the officers, there must have been blood on the floor somewhere and I stepped in it."

"You couldn't have stepped in it outside?"

"I hadn't thought of that."

"Think of it now."

"I guess I could have. As far as that goes, I could have stepped in it anywhere, couldn't I?"

"You tell me."

"I said it must have been in the house, because that's what I thought they meant. If a body was in the house, then the blood was in the house."

The attorney was studying him, nodded, and jotted something down. "Okay."

"I guess I sound stupid."

"No, you sound like you're telling the truth."

Johnny felt much better about his situation until the attorney had been gone for about an hour. Then it came to him that being in here was like being in another world. Only visitors were your hope. There was no open doorway.

At 9:30 p.m. he had a cola and three cigarettes and was led to his room again, where, despite a subdued fear that buzzed through him like a high electronic moan, he felt sleep coming on, and he was grateful for it. He hoped it lasted the night.

3

Singing and Secrets

WHEN MRS. DUNBAR REMEMBERED THE CURRENT UGLINESS, SHE felt immediately agitated, unequal to rising and meeting the day. A piece of sunlight, whose source she couldn't determine, lay precisely in the center of an embroidered blue flower on her bedspread. It was a pleasant sight and she watched it until her body rallied to morning. Age was an inconvenience, but could be dealt with. She got up, made her bed, took a careful shower. She recalled the quick readiness of youth, when a shower and facing the day was a mindless dash. Not so now. Careful. If ever she broke a bone, she might never rise again. She didn't like wearing skirts anymore, because the increasing curve of her spine made the front hem dip lower than in the back, an imbalanced and unattractive appearance. She didn't mind seeing women wear slacks in church, and more and more often did so herself, but today she would be speaking with the rector. The nature of the talk required more formal, respectful attire. She donned her one black skirt, a rose blouse—she wasn't a nun—that was slightly too large and thus would accommodate a misshapen back, stockings, and black, low-heeled shoes. She applied a touch of Tangee lipstick and quickly twisted her long white hair into a figure eight and pinned it firmly in place. A white curl loosened at the top of the roll. She considered whacking the stray off with one snip of scissors, but she was in a hurry. She let it go.

Her mother had been deft with scissors—could snip in two a wasp on the wing. She could also fix her own sewing machine, because as a young girl she'd worked in a factory and couldn't make quota if she had a breakdown and had to wait for the mechanic.

Mrs. Dunbar looked up the address of the new county jail, and drove around that particular city block four times. She believed jails should not be in the town itself, but then how would safe transportation be possible if the building itself were a long distance from the courts? That would be begging trouble. Hitchhiking burglars, rapists, murderers? *Overdoing Letitia*, she admonished herself. *Calm does it better. Besides, the town isn't large enough for many violent crimes.* Now that she knew where the entrance and exits to the jail complex were, she felt less overwhelmed by the idea of it. The building was modern, predominantly brick, much like a bank. It probably had elevators, air conditioning, television. Johnny might be more comfortable there than at his own place, which, according to Zeena, was a "rathole."

Mrs. Dunbar headed for the church. That was familiar territory, and she believed the car itself drove smoother with the new destination, all the ruts and curves having been retained in the metal memory.

She had never visited the rector, Father Madison. Church was one thing. Church *offices* were another. She didn't believe in them. This had been her husband's church. Her own was more . . . lowly. A little more emotionally engaged. No dancing in the aisles or speaking in tongues, but joyful singing, babies wailing. Pie crust and grape juice for communion. The members weren't low class so much as peasantry. The elders and deacons were farmers, and their contributions to the plate often meant their families went without something. As a child, she had admired the church men, but as an adult wondered if their duty weren't misplaced. How could being charitable reduce the poverty of one's family? By feeling generous? Maybe so. Maybe assuaging another's physical hunger assuaged your own. She doubted God kept minor balances in mind.

She waited in the rector's office and chatted briefly with Rosie, his secretary, whom she knew from services and whom she liked. Rosie had an incorrigible five-year old who yelled Amen or Hallelujah sporadically, but especially in quiet moments. At least it was an appropriate word. It injected a little passion in the building.

"I remember Luke," Rosie said. "It's pretty hard to miss him. Was."

"So you were here when he sang with the choir?"

"Yes. I had been here for, let's see, I don't know. A few months at least. That was a couple of years ago, right?"

"Three, I think. Late summer, like now. About your age, wasn't he? And a good-looking fellow?"

"Uh huh. I noticed him. But he wasn't one for responsibility." She glanced at the group of photos on her desk, all of her son. "A woman can usually tell that."

Mrs. Dunbar agreed, though she didn't say so. Most women knew the nature of man they dealt with. Unfortunately, some stayed with a dangerous man because they didn't know where else to turn and didn't want to be alone. A woman's world could be a frightening place. For a certain kind of woman. Rosie was a wise little thing.

The rector came to the front office for her. "Letitia," he said, genuine surprise evident in his expression. "What are you doing here on a weekday? Is anything wrong?"

"Of course," she said. "Or I wouldn't be here."

With the door closed behind them, and Father Madison fully attentive on his side of the desk, Mrs. Dunbar told him about her great-nephew's plight. "What I really need, though, if you can help, is information about the young man who was killed."

"The Michaels boy?"

"Yes."

"Very sad. He was so young." He bowed his head briefly, as if in recollection.

Mrs. Dunbar suspected he was praying. It seemed natural and genuine, so she was touched. If it had seemed the least bit ostentatious, she would have been offended. She might even stop attending this church if phoniness was in the nature of its head officer. Head meaning other than God.

"Do you know anything about his death?" He was looking at her again.

"I know Johnny didn't do it."

"Then why was he arrested?"

"Because they've made a mistake. Johnny's not an angel by any means, but I don't think he did this. And he *said* he didn't. He's not good at lying. I came here because the Michaels boy sang with our choir a few times, and I thought we might know something about him or have a tape of him. I remember that at least one performance was taped." She had a picture in her mind of a blond-haired young man, very handsome. One corner of his mouth pulled down when he hit high notes. It made him look like a Dickens' choir boy. A very thin one, with eyes raised to heaven.

"I don't know anything about him," the rector said. "But Betty Miles might. He came into the choir through her, I think. Then he began attending services. I don't remember the particulars very well." He swiveled his chair, looked on the bookshelf directly behind him, swung back. "I imagine we do have a video of him somewhere, and maybe more than one. Betty usually has someone tape the choir performances."

"I thought she did. Do you think I could borrow the videos? They are for all of us, aren't they?"

"You know, Letitia, I'm not sure. It hasn't come up before. They're part of the church records, a history of our activities. We could use them, I suppose, in celebrations, maybe as memorials. As I said, it hasn't come up." His dark brows drew together in a quite charming way. She believed he was trying to be fatherly. "Why do you want them?" he asked. "That's probably the deciding factor."

"Because I don't have the slightest idea how to help Johnny. But I did remember Luke Michaels singing here, and I did remember that we recorded at least one of those performances. So, if I follow my natural inclinations, I'll examine the performances. It's a start. Maybe it will be all I can do."

"What could you possibly learn?"

"Probably nothing. But I would feel *useful*."

She saw him relent—a positive nod to himself. He patted the edge of the desk blotter. "Okay," he said. "It couldn't do any harm. Now," he turned the chair around, glanced at the bookcases behind him, swiveled again, leaned to look at shelves a few feet down. Then he got up and began searching more closely.

Mrs. Dunbar, still seated, examined the room, too, looking for the tapes but also assessing the rector's office. The drapes were open and afternoon light slanted into the room, across the desk. Books, books, and books, even stacked on the floor like high rises of another world, indicated an active, inquiring mind. Everything was old-world, warm and charming: a worn, low footstool covered in burgundy brocade, a slender, round table on which a candle burned before photos of various individuals, likely his family; two silk-shaded lamps, adding a diffuse golden glow to the polished wood. He liked nice things. And he was a collector—of miniatures. Brass dogs and cats grouped at the end of one shelf; birds at another; horse-drawn carriages; tiny automobiles.

"You should build a scale village," she said.

"What?" He turned and she gestured at the shelves. "You carve miniatures. You might enjoy building a village. I've seen some wonderful ones, especially when I was a girl. Some were so quaint and beautiful that I wanted to live there. I wanted to be small, actually, and fit into that world—not find one my own size."

"I know what you're talking about. I've seen them, too." For a second he seemed wistful, then shrugged that thought away, and smiled at her. "You hit the nail on the head. Letitia. I've always wanted to carve, paint, maybe sculpt or make pottery. Something with my hands. A friend of mine, at seminary, wanted to be a cobbler. He wanted to make shoes." He shook his head. "There's no livelihood in that occupation, not in the modern world."

"There might be in designing shoes. I'm too fond of shoes. Italian shoes, especially."

"He wanted to make them, hands on leather, not just on paper." He turned, took a figure from a shelf and handed it to Mrs. Dunbar. "I did this."

It was a wooden squirrel, the body no more than two inches and the tail curving up and over its back, and there a bit to the side, as though in mid-switch. With one fingertip Mrs. Dunbar traced the beautiful lines. "You captured the mischief," she said. "And even the quickness. It's really well done."

He handed another one to her. A dog, curled into a crescent, eyes imploring, the tip of the tail a little comma-question.

"They're beautiful," she said. "You should indulge your talent as often as possible."

"Carving takes time. And it's dangerous for the clumsy. I nick myself."

"I noticed the bandage."

"Oh, that." He looked at the skin-colored adhesive strip between thumb and forefinger on his left hand. "I had a guard on that hand, but I found the one open spot."

"The squirrel alone is worth it."

"Thank you." He took the carvings from her carefully, put them in place. He glanced out the window toward the parking lot, rose hurriedly, speaking as he did so. "I'll ask Rosie about the videos," he said, and left the room.

Mrs. Dunbar, following his glance, saw a flash of yellow, and recognized Betty Miles closing a car door. Betty headed toward the parish house. She was an attractive woman, slender, dressed in a yellow sundress and red shoes. Her blonde hair was kept short, wavy and thick, and always in place. Chic and controlled. Very nice. Mrs. Dunbar thought the rector and Betty might make a good couple and suspected the relationship was already under way. Suddenly, in the frame of now, while the rector and Betty were in proximity in this place and in her mind, Mrs. Dunbar believed they were already involved. The way he had said the name Betty Miles, was, she recalled, oddly paced—the "Miles" tacked on as an afterthought and in a different tone. "Betty" had been his first, soft response.

Reflection could be wrong, but it often construed a different, and more accurate path for thought. The two people had already found each other. Well, good for them, she supposed. Good.

She dropped her gaze and the sight of her own hands, the skin almost transparent and the blue veins too visible, reminded her that her own pretty days were past. She had never been beautiful, but the man she had loved had found her so.

"We've got them, Letitia," the rector said from the hallway. He was holding a cup with the printed message "God approves of coffee." Right behind him was Rosie, a stack of videos in arm. "Don't let these out of your possession," the rector continued. "I want to be responsible just in case it comes up later on."

"I'd feel the same way." Mrs. Dunbar put them in a plastic bag. "I'll get them back tomorrow morning if I can. No later than tomorrow afternoon."

"That'll be fine." He retreated into his office, which surprised Mrs. Dunbar. Surely he had seen Betty arriving. Why didn't he wait to greet her?

"Thanks, Rosie." Mrs. Dunbar patted the bag.

"Sure. Enjoy. Rewind them, please. People forget now, since DVDs don't have to be rewound."

"I'll be sure to rewind them." She didn't know anything about DVDs. Not yet.

In the patio, Mrs. Dunbar saw Betty before a half-barrel planter filled with brilliant red geraniums, looking at her watch. "I wish I had a camera," Mrs. Dunbar said. "That would make a lovely picture."

Her words startled the other woman. "They are beautiful this year. Who did them?"

"Myra Wren," Mrs. Dunbar said, noting that Betty was not cheerful at all, despite the colorful clothing and some artfully applied makeup. "She's an artist with flowers. Like you are with music."

"That's kind."

"And true. I wasn't talking about photographing only the flowers, though. I meant you and your dress, the patio, the sunlight."

"Oh. Thanks again. It's an outfit I don't wear often. Few appropriate places, you know."

"I think most places would be appropriate." Mrs. Dunbar indicated the red shoes. "I would wear those myself, if I were young."

"Really?"

"Yes."

"You should wear them anyhow, then. It's never too late." She glanced toward the parish house expectantly. "You have a pleasant day, Mrs. Dunbar."

"You, too."

Mrs. Dunbar went on to her car, aware of her awkward passage but not embarrassed. She was grateful she was mobile. She missed snazzy shoes. She would wear nicer ones if she were straight bodied. Doing so now would be torture of herself and of anyone watching her. Or comic relief.

The plastic bag, stamped with the logo of a national department store, filled with a breeze and fluttered against her wrist. Having the videos excited her a little. She was on the brink of discovery. This was a feeling she appreciated but didn't misinterpret. Staying busy was sometimes all a person could do.

When she drove by the jail, she thought of Johnny in there, sweet boy. She remembered him falling asleep at a Thanksgiving dinner. He was on a chair, boosted up even more by two phone books. With elbow on the table, hand against his cheek, he fell asleep repeatedly. He was supposed to eat his asparagus. Mrs. Dunbar had openly taken his side. She had speared the asparagus pieces with her fork, popped them in her mouth and ate them. Her niece-in-law had had the grace to look a bit ashamed. Johnny was allowed to go to his room then. Of course, he didn't go there. He sneaked out front, and fell asleep under the porch swing.

* * *

Father Madison didn't know how to take Betty Miles. She was one of the prettiest women he'd ever seen, and he liked the sheer precision of her. Her body lines were nice. He had read once that some women had the right frame for modeling, and she did. Clothes softened on her, draped clean and graceful. She was a woman who could wear a suit or slacks or, maybe, even a terry robe, and look proper and alluring, too. But she wasn't right for him. There was a sultriness about her at times, as if another nature came to the surface. Not another personality—no crazy multi personality or anything—just a tinge of . . . sordidness. Maybe, he admitted, he was attracted to that very thing even while he deplored it.

He thought of her clear bell voice. Lovely. That, too, very clean. One of his responsibilities was to oversee the worship music, but he preferred to allow someone with a gift in that area to choose.

He took from the shelf the miniature squirrel Letitia Dunbar had admired. If he were a different man, he would be a craftsman. He would get booths at fairs and at some of the permanent artists' venues, like Arrow Rock, Blackwater, Missouri Town, or just a small shop on Fourth Avenue. He lived poor anyhow—took very little salary, and turned most of that back to the Lord's work in one way or the other. Instantly, he felt a deep sadness at even the thought of leaving the ministry. No. Never. This was his calling. That thought brought a sensation of peace. *Thank you.*

Replacing the wooden creature, he opened his office door, left it ajar and, from a short distance away, peered out. Rosie was speaking to someone, smiling, and then Betty came into view, her eyes seeking his. She came inside, closed the door behind her as she had begun to do, as though their conversations might become intimate. They had already been very private, secret, he supposed. Inexplicably, he delighted in her presence.

* * *

Watching the videos was a pleasant self-assignment, more enjoyable than watching a movie. Mrs. Dunbar knew these people, at least by sight, but now saw them in a new light, in a kind of mystery. She looked at Myra Wren a number of times because she liked Myra and only now noticed how very pallid the woman was. She realized that the choir, in general, was old. Only a few young people participated, and then not regularly—Anne Mercer, Molly Robeson, Rosie, and Leroy Atkins. When the camera first caught the director, Betty Miles, the woman was smiling shyly and Mrs. Dunbar was again struck by her delicate beauty. Betty herself was a singer, though she usually directed the choir. She had a few special-music solos during church events. Mrs. Dunbar recalled especially "Here I Am, Lord." Was it possible to sing such a song without conviction of the truth it represented? Mrs. Dunbar didn't think so. Of course, a conviction, even a deep desire, could be temporary or, at least, not constant. Humans weren't constant.

On the third tape, Luke Michaels was in the choir, and Mrs. Dunbar became slightly breathless and guilty, as if she were spying on someone. She played it twice, often losing her concentration by thinking that this young man was no longer alive. What was she looking for, anyway? Maybe this was a pointless and even cold endeavor. But her self-deprecation led to a sharper focus on the victim. She noted that even among so many other singers, Luke attracted attention, and not because his voice could be heard. He was one of many. But he was truly striking, and there was an intensity about him, as if he were aware every moment of an audience, and was deliberately upstaging the other singers. His eyes sent the message, "Here, here. Look at me."

Mrs. Dunbar wrote down the counter-numbers marking Luke's appearances on the tape. He had sung with the choir during seven performances—more than any of the other young people. Someone was usually missing. The tapes had made him more real to her. They had also verified her memory: he could sing, but his arrogance projected as much as his voice. Some choir members seemed at times to have shared her feelings about him. Two rolled their eyes. Another mugged a downward smile. During one of Luke's solos, Anne Mercer kept her head slightly bowed. No one else did that.

Mrs. Dunbar went on her porch to breathe fresh air and listen to the hum of life, cars in the distance, a wasp too nearby, an angry jay and an angrier squirrel. It seemed wrong to dislike someone who was dead. Luke Michaels had had a short upper lip. That thought, she knew, was apropos of nothing, except that standards of beauty or standards in general rarely encompassed reality. People who were homely by some standard usually knew it. They compensated with whatever arsenal they had. She strolled down her front walk, picked up a rubber band so no bird would get it. Paperboys—and girls—worked too hard and were too young to know rubber bands were dangerous. Johnny had failed as a paperboy. He had on three occasions, one of them Christmas Eve, dumped all his papers in the creek about a mile behind his home. The first time, he concocted a story about his bike falling off the bridge. The other times he just presented his impassive countenance and gave no explanation at all. He would lie and evade when pressured. A person could have a bad trait, even more than one, and still be good.

"And vice versa," she announced. Great leaders often had the greatest flaws. There wasn't a great person who would rise totally blameless from close scrutiny. Much was relative. She thought of Martha, sister of Mary, who labored in the kitchen while Mary lolled at Jesus's feet. The standard interpretation of that was not her interpretation. But—Jesus was good, Mary was good, and Martha, bless her scrub-worn hands and servant heart, was good. Better.

Mrs. Dunbar's mother often said that God wasn't hesitant to admit He made mistakes and wasn't hesitant to correct them either. He was also open to arguments.

She went back inside, slipped the last tape in the machine, pushed play, aligned the picture and, before she could sit down, was stunned still. A high clang of many cymbals, and a voice screaming a sustained note, slammed her dizzy. Something deep and heavy thrummed in her lungs. She was inhaling sound. She muted the video. With eyes wide open and wary she settled back. Luke Michaels, wearing strips of black leather, pointed a finger right at her, his lips pursed as if saying "youuuuuuu." It was so coarse, ugly. Then the picture broadened to include the periphery and two other musicians, dressed in leather pants, but the whole cloth. Their leather vests were atop tee shirts. She was relieved. Even Luke wasn't as close to nude as it first appeared.

Mrs. Dunbar released the mute but also lowered the volume. Melody rather than screech reigned. The singer was still Luke Michaels, the young man who now would not be singing ever again, would not be living his life. This performance was not really outrageous, just a young band, for a different audience. She wasn't a prude. Luke had wanted to shock the listener not only with the beauty and power of his voice, but of his body and person. That was a common goal in the young. *See me*, they said. *Know me as individual.*

* * *

Acting on Andy's suggestion, Galway didn't ask for a private consultation room, but went to the regular waiting room, where, despite the newness of the place, and the sturdy maintenance budget, the area was grimy and littered—at best. The tall metal ashtray just outside the door was overflowing, and cigarettes had been squashed into the tile of the waiting room. Empty and half-empty soda cans were on the low window sill—a window with wire mesh striating the glass. A thin small man, somewhere between eighteen and forty, said, "guess this was an over-night camp ground for hoboes."

"Looks like," Galway said. "Though I have a fondness for hoboes."

The man squinted to see if Galway was serious, then nodded. "So do I really. Not hoboes then." He continued squinting, then relaxed his features, shrugged. "I can't think of another category. How about slobs?"

"Good. That crosses boundaries."

The man nodded briskly, very pleased at the encounter. They had both come off well. "I'm visiting my wife," he said.

"I'm sorry."

That gained another nod. The man moved over by the door leading to the inner building. First in line.

Galway filled out the visitor's form. Under "Relationship" he checked "Friend." He knew this might make the prosecutors view him as a hostile witness, but then they might recognize his name, and if not, they'd learn soon enough. Meanwhile, he wasn't an attorney in this world, just a friend of the family. He was allowed to carry nothing in with him, not even pencil and paper, but had to empty his pockets into a small cloth-covered wire basket.

A woman had entered and filled out the form quickly, without looking at anyone. The officer put her before Galway, and the three visitors trooped in, single file. The other two went straight ahead behind a deputy, but Galway was taken through another pressure-locked door, and entered a different visitation room. This one was divided into cubicles. Maximum security.

He sat down, watched the inner door.

He had never been in this particular part of the system. He had been where the other visitors had been led. There, inmates and visitors sat on either side of a counter, with unbreakable glass between then, and talked through phone receivers. They could see one another's expressions and could even whisper, so it wasn't totally dehumanizing. An abused person, for example, could feel physically safe while visiting the abuser, and perhaps even feel a little power, since leaving was an option. It still allowed intimacy and privacy, to a degree. Locked doors were locked doors, however, and Galway had still felt temporarily a prisoner. Someone else had the key and thus someone else held his freedom as hostage to good behavior on both their parts. This part of the system was worse. Single glass cells surrounded by steel.

A deputy opened the door on the other side, nodded at Galway and stepped back into the hall, making way for Johnny to enter. He wore a terribly wrinkled, vivid orange jumpsuit, much too big, white socks, and orange, slip-on, rubber shoes. To people of some sensibilities, Galway thought, the clothing alone was a punishment. Looking at it was, too. Johnny's red hair, too curly for order in the best of care, was matted and flat on one side, as if he had slept a long time. The guard shut the door. With an awkward walk, somewhat shyly, Johnny came to the counter and slipped into the chair. Galway nodded at the receiver and the boy took it down, held it to his ear. He seemed embarrassed by the whole situation, but anxious to please, like a kid hoping for adoption.

"Hello Johnny. I'm Galway Evans."

"Yeah. Mr. Fielding told me you'd come by. You're on my case, too." He grinned. "Not in a bad way, though. Not like my mom's on my case."

Galway approved of the formal title for Andy and he appreciated the play on words, though the young man shouldn't be in too playful a mood. "I am. But I'm on it primarily because I'm a friend of Mrs. Dunbar's."

"You're a friend of Aunt Lettie's? Cool." He seemed to remember the situation. "I guess it's cool."

"Why don't you tell me what happened that got you in here?"

"I told Mr. Fielding."

"I know. And I've read the police report. I just want to hear it all in your words."

"What did the report say?"

"I imagine you already know that."

"I just wanted to hear how *you* read it."

His smile was really nice, a little gap-toothed and restrained. He had just been witty in circumstances where most people, particularly innocent ones, might have been a little more subdued. "Okay," Galway said. "So, you ready now?"

"Yeah." He looked at the door on Galway's side of the glass. "I didn't do anything," he said. "I'd like to get the hell out of here."

"You at least burglarized a dwelling."

"Uh huh. But I didn't kill anybody. I didn't even *see* Luke. They say he was there, dead, when I was in the house. That's spooky as hell."

"How could you miss seeing the body?"

"I don't know. I checked the house out, looked in every room. I did it pretty fast but he couldn't have been there. Unless he was hiding." He broke eye contact, spoke to the table. "If Luke was there, for all I know the guy who killed him was there, too. When

I was, you know? He may have been watching me all the time." He shrugged. "Spooky shit."

"Michaels was a friend of yours, wasn't he? Why burglarize a friend?"

"He isn't—wasn't—really a friend. And he had a lot of stuff. There's a good market for recording equipment. I didn't go for anything big. Just some microphones and a digital recorder and a little mixer. I had planned to take the soundboard but it was too big for the window."

"Was it for you?"

"It was for money."

"You knew what kind of equipment he had?"

"Sure. Everybody does. Did. He recorded all the time. The guys talked."

"What guys?"

"Musicians. People that party at his place."

"You one of the partiers?"

"Not regular. I've been there a couple of times. I like to listen. You know. I don't play anything. Play the radio." He laughed a little, sad laugh. "My dad says that."

"Why did you think Luke wouldn't be home Saturday night?"

"Something." Johnny stared at his hands. They were long, bony, and freckled. They looked deft and competent, at odds with his unkempt person. "I can't remember. You know. Not a big thing. It was a Saturday. He's gone most Friday and Saturday nights, playing somewhere."

"Where?"

"Usually at the Boondocks. He's out there pretty often, plays with different groups. Same musicians, usually, just different names. Why does that matter? He obviously wasn't at a gig. He was in the house dead. That's what I hear."

"Yes he was. Maybe someone else was in there with him, or had been. One of the musicians."

"Nah," he shook his head. "Not one of them."

The reaction was very quick, protective.

"Why did you hang around after you left the house?"

"Did I?"

"You were seen, Johnny, parked on the street."

"I wanted to watch Luke come home."

"Why?"

"I don't know."

"To see if someone came home with him?"

No answer. Eyes down and to the side.

"Who were you looking for?"

"Nobody in particular. I was curious. Maybe I was going to put the stuff I took back."

"Really?"

"Yeah. I think so."

"Okay," Galway said. "Anything else?"

"I didn't do it. That's my else."

"And that's a good one." The boy was trying to be brave when it probably wasn't a big part of his nature. Galway understood that feeling, trying to be better than you were. "Okay," he said. "How about you give me the names of the music crowd, the people Luke plays with? Then your aunt and I will see what we can do."

"Aunt Lettie's helping you?"

"Whether I want her to or not."

Johnny laughed. "That's a good one, too. She'll stay on you."

"You might call her. She's worried about you."

"You got a cigarette?"

"No, but I'll get you some."

"I don't want to ask Mom and Aunt Lettie. They wouldn't get them anyhow. And I don't want to bum. Not in here. I don't get to mix. Only murderer they got."

"I'll get some for you."

"How tall are you, anyway?"

"Six five."

"I thought so. Even sitting down, you're way up there. It must feel good to be that big. People pay attention when you talk."

"Nope. Doesn't work that way. First, I'm not big, just tall. Second, size doesn't mean anything unless it's used in the right way. If you can't do anything right, you're just a big mistake."

"I know how that feels."

"I can help you, Johnny, if you're telling me the truth."

Outside the visiting room, Galway asked a deputy how to leave cigarettes or other items for a prisoner. He often asked questions of a person in charge just as a matter of courtesy and good rapport. But this place really was foreign to him. It had been completed only a year or so ago. The old one had been a crumbling wooden structure, so casual that inmates were allowed often to take a break outside, or cook something in the kitchen. The ground level had been the sheriff's residence for years. The sheriff's wife cooked for the inmates, and did the laundry. In hot weather, the main doors were left open, and even the wood-framed screen doors were unlatched. It was the country home of misbehaving good guys. There was, though, a double-wood door always locked between the downstairs and the upstairs, and the rooms upstairs had regular cell doors, bars and locks.

Galway drove to a convenience mart, bought a carton of a decent brand, had the clerk put it in a brown paper bag. He took it back to the jail, borrowed a pen from the visiting room receptionist or clerk—she was in a uniform only slightly different from the deputies. He wrote across the folded-down bag, "Mr. John Rowland."

She was watching him, so he didn't have to rap on the window. "Will this get to him?"

She fiddled with levers at the edges of the window, and then slid the lower part up to give access to the metal tray at the bottom. "Sure. They'll be checked first, so he won't get them right away."

"Can I leave money for him, too?"

"Yes. You'll have to sign a receipt and I'll have to get my supervisor for that."

"Why is this visitor's room in such bad shape?"

"The crews follow a schedule. They're assigned parts of the complex and specific hours. Varying the schedule could cause a bad mix-up. Night crew didn't get here last night, and the next crew isn't due until late afternoon." She smiled. She had very full lips, a dark lipstick, almost brown, and a restrained smile that threatened to be gorgeous, if fully released. Her hair line was far back on her wide brow, and it reminded him of photos he had seen of Nefertiti. What a glow in this dimness.

When Galway left, Johnny had thirty dollars to his credit, not much Galway imagined, for junk food.

The receptionist had improved his impression of the place.

Galway headed downtown. He had to meet Andy for lunch.

Johnny Rowland, meanwhile, was escorted back to his slit of a cell in his own special pod. No snacks, no magazines. No smokes. Nothing. He felt like an insect.

He trusted this Galway guy. His Aunt Lettie was a strange woman anyhow, and this was to her credit, he thought. A person's friends, as his mother often said, defined him.

He sat on the edge of his metal bed, hands clasped loosely between his knees. If he got out of this, if he got out of this . . . He choked back the urge to cry, flexed his fingers, and took a deep breath. He didn't want to die. It couldn't lead to anything good—a blank space, especially for him, who had no good deeds to tally up, if that is, good deeds counted at all. No faith in anything.

* * *

"I think the kid is telling the truth," Andy said. "But he *may* have done it. He's a little naïve, but he's bright enough. He could be a talented liar. I've known many of them. It doesn't matter as far as our representing him, of course."

"Yes, it does. For me."

"I know."

"Have you contacted his folks?" Galway asked.

"Not yet. He doesn't want me to."

"Then I'll cover your fee."

"I've already appeared with him for the arraignment. I couldn't get court-appointed even if I wanted to, since they're assigning almost all those cases to Murdoch in Higginsville."

"What about bond?"

"He doesn't want to be bailed out."

"Then let me pay your fee. You know I've got the money."

"Tell you what, Galway, if he's guilty, you pay half my time. If not, it's free."

"I pay half your time no matter the result."

"Okay. Done."

"Good. If Johnny *did* do it, then I've really made the right changes in my life, because my instincts are wrong. And being an attorney, as you know, is largely instinct."

"*Partly* instinct," Andy said. "Largely knowledge of the law."

Galway looked toward the smoking section, only two tables away. "The thin gray line," he said, and breathed deeply, as if inhaling the smoke. He would have, if he'd been nearer. If he had a choice of standing by a non-smoker and a polluter, he chose the latter. He liked the smell, and the taste, and the act. He was a smoker bred. But he had quit.

"Go ahead, have a cigarette. You don't have to change every iota of your life to get a fresh start. Be a smoker."

"Nope. I gave that up." Galway cut into his steak. "I'm surprised, actually, that Johnny Rowland could even steal. He seems too . . . maybe innocent. He's young minded. At his age, I was going into law school. Not willingly, though." He regretted saying that. Andy already knew it. Besides it was time to eradicate old grievances. His parents were dead now. They had wanted him to be successful. They urged him to do his best and expected him to be the best at most of his endeavors. So he was. But not from his own desire. He had had an inordinate desire to please his parents. They had been more engrossed in each other than in him, or so it seemed.

"Johnny's not slow," Galway said. "He's actually sort of winning. I'm positive he couldn't kill anybody unless he was backed into a corner."

"Maybe he was. In Luke Michaels' bedroom."

"On the other hand, maybe he's protecting someone. The innocent minded are perfect protectors. They think the ideal is worth dying for."

"He's not an idealist, Galway. You are."

"I'm a cynic."

"You're struggling. You'll get through it."

Galway nodded. He doubted he would ever feel differently. He couldn't allow some memories because sorrow tagged along and then overwhelmed him. He had to think of small, immediate actions, pleasures of the moment. Now. Tomorrow. Keep the hands so busy the mind didn't dare wander.

* * *

"Luke Michaels looks a lot younger than I expected," Galway said to Mrs. Dunbar. "He certainly sought the camera." He punched the rewind button. He appreciated choir music, but he wasn't listening so much as looking and that required a reining of attention. "How many tapes did you listen to? How many hours?"

"The Michaels boy is only on some of each tape. I fast-forwarded much of it. And I listened with patience. It's good music, Galway."

"I know that. I'm not complaining. I wonder about an eternity of it, though. You know. God." He watched her as he spoke, and sure enough, her eyes snapped to him. He grinned. "You think there are tryouts?"

"Probably right now. He's always listening, I imagine."

"Not to me." Galway had embarrassed himself. "I didn't mean that." He put in the next tape. "What's the cue number for this one?"

"Start at the beginning. There's a real nice solo by Luke."

It *was* good. The melody was simple and pleasing. The choir hummed behind Luke for part of the song, joined in on one line: "*Let me love in your shadow.*" At its end, Galway glanced at Mrs. Dunbar. "Again?"

"No. I listened to it twice earlier. I get sidetracked because I know these people."

Sometime later, when Galway put in the last tape, Mrs. Dunbar said, "I'll be back in a minute," and, cane not really touching the floor, left him alone.

He pushed "play."

Sound exploded, harsh and unmelodic, a high vocal screech barely distinguishable from guitar strings bending notes to piercing level. Then the sound stopped, absolutely, and started again, softer, the instruments background for recognizable lyrics sung in a good voice. A trio. Pretty good. Luke the leader.

Mrs. Dunbar reentered the room.

"You listened to this, I guess," Galway said.

"After I recovered from the opening."

"I don't doubt it. It's a wonder he and the others weren't deaf. What did you think of that outfit?"

"There's more to it than first meets the eye, thank goodness."

Galway thought Michaels' voice would have more emotional power if the listener couldn't see him. Michaels was too pretentious in every tape. It wasn't so much his expression while singing, but his natural demeanor. His eyebrows appeared permanently slightly raised, as if he were born to disdain. Galway believed people were pretty much the outcome of their genes and something amiss showed in Michaels' features.

Mrs. Dunbar made a few observations about the young people. Once she walked to the screen and identified a woman with a touch of her finger. "That's Myra Wren," she said. "The woman you worked for, the one who told you about Luke."

"I thought I recognized her," Galway said. "Is there something I should know about her?"

"What I told you—she's a friend of mine."

"Oh," he said. "Done." He assumed that if ever that lady were in distress, he was to rush to the rescue. And he would, if he could.

* * *

Galway never closed the drapes in his own living room, and now, with no lamps on, moonlight shifted across the floor and furniture as though it were itself a cloud, a delicate substance. His cell phone emitted a short musical note, too airy for his mood, but welcome. He clicked on the text message icon. From Walter Hildy.

At 2 tomorrow, you, me, and Sheriff B if he can make it. Keep it quiet.

He had come to appreciate text messages. They were less personal, didn't trigger memories as quickly or intimately as did a voice, and didn't require immediate response.

He was going to see the inside of the victim's house. He approached the idea cautiously. Instead of dread, he felt a tinge of excitement and allowed that to grow. He had always enjoyed the discovery of truth, even when it was against his own client's case, and that might be the case here. He believed that each side should know everything the opposing side had, from the beginning. He understood, though, that truth was relative, and that wit and drama could make good seem bad and bad seem good. Sometimes divulging a fact caused an injustice. Ultimately, a person's conscience probably should be respected more than the law, but law applied to all and conscience varied. So—an ethical and moral man could feel guilty following letter of the law.

Moonlight had found a resting place in the room beyond, at the inner frame of an open French door to the dining room. It shifted a little, blurred, and if he were a different type of person, he might think it a visiting presence. He would welcome a comforting belief of any kind. He rubbed his face. Tomorrow he would do something new. In the morning, a little sleuthing. In the afternoon, the murder scene.

As he went upstairs to bed, he remembered the yapping dog, the fiery Pomeranian with a mistress who couldn't stroke the little pet as she once had.

4

Musicians' Arte

AT 9:45 A.M. THURSDAY MORNING, GALWAY DROVE TO SOUTH Fourth Avenue. The area was generally known as Fair Street, because for one weekend in spring and fall the sidewalks, streets, alleys, patios, and some buildings were filled with artists, craftspeople, poets, musicians, and appreciative audiences. The rest of the year, the quaint stores and restaurants drew a small but faithful stream of patrons and performers. Galway had only attended the fair a couple of times. His mother had valued crafts. She believed herself to be absolutely untalented, with no imagination and no practical skills. But she supported artists by buying their work and, if she didn't want to keep it, by giving it away. He thought she might have been a good dancer and imagined she danced for his father, when he, Galway, wasn't around. He had come down from bed one summer evening, not able to sleep. He was eight or nine. He had heard music coming from their bedroom, and had opened the door. His mother was holding an orange and red scarf across her breasts, and other scarves, myriad colors, hung from a gold cord around her lower hips. She was barefoot. Her hair was loose, straight, and a long strand fell on each side of her face, making it appear long and thin, a stranger's face.

"You wicked thing," she said, but she didn't sound angry. He had felt much an outsider. Maybe all kids did at some point. They sensed the mystery behind the relationship of two people so totally different. Love. An inexplicable bond.

His father had led him back into the hallway, up the stairs, and kept him company a short time, advising him gently to knock before entering a bedroom. Any room for that matter.

Fair Street was like a tiny country of its own. Some storefronts had awnings, or recessed windows or doors, planters with flowers, or a small tree, a dart board, a table just big enough for a chess game. Art work. Dresses. Young people.

By a bookstore entrance a table held stacks of paperbacks and a handwritten sign—"Read for Free." Galway read a few of the titles, smiled, and, when a young man appeared in the doorway, said, "This is a different sales approach."

"It's like day-old bread," the man said.

"Don't they get taken?"

"Sometimes. Who's going to worry about someone who steals a used book?"

"I'll be back," Galway said.

"You do that, sir."

Galway noted the name of the store. He planned to do some business here. "I'm looking for a music store, where someone might know about local bands."

"Across the street and half a block more in the direction you're headed."

In a few minutes, Galway found the Musicians' Arte, and stepped inside a cool, shadowy, long room filled with instruments, racks of song books, sheet music, and other music paraphernalia, and filled also with the husky sound of blues at low volume, Tom Waits' "Whistlin Past the Graveyard."

In the back, not visible, someone picked a guitar, hesitantly, a scale that must sound pathetic to the student if the front room blues carried back there.

"May I help you?" An olive-skinned, pleasant-faced young man came forward. He was dressed in baggy denims, an over-sized blue shirt with sleeves so long the rolled cuffs still came past his wrist bones, and a blue cap sporting a single quarter-note logo. He had an almost cherub friendliness about him.

"You carry anything by local bands?"

"These." He pointed at the glass counter nearby. On the top shelf, CDs were propped up, angled like photographs. "Do you know which group you want?" The young man walked behind the counter.

"Fallen Angels, for one. I'm open, though, to talent."

"The Angels are good. Or they *were* good. Actually, the best group for instrumentals, not just vocals, is Daring Do, an all-girl band."

"Nice name."

"Yep. Nice group, too. They switch instruments around. Together they got fiddle, autoharp, banjo, mouth-harp, mandolin, guitar and bass. Sometimes other stuff." He smiled. "I'm the brother of the fiddler. She does mandolin and guitar, too, when needed."

"You sold me. If they have a CD, I'll take it."

"They have three. The Fallen Angels have two." He took five CDs from the display, handed them to Galway. "You really want them all?"

"I do." Galway read the Daring Do credits and admired the photo. The instruments were as lovely as the ladies. "Nice," he said. "I like old-time music. Appalachian especially."

"They do some Appalachian, mostly the Irish heritage tunes, but they're not limited. You have to hear them. They're bluegrass, blues, soft rock. Look at their other labels."

"Versatile group."

"Are you a detective?"

Galway liked the clerk, who was apparently not only sensitive but also direct. The cap made him even more boyish, as if he had just donned it, to head outside and play.

"No, I'm not. I guess you've heard about Luke Michaels? I noticed you said the Fallen Angels *were* a band. Past tense."

"Everyone's heard about Luke. And the band was falling apart before that."

"Why?"

"Who are you to know?"

Whoa! The street wasn't as friendly as he thought. "I'm an attorney, or former attorney. The man they've arrested for the murder is related to a friend of mine. I'm finding out what I can. I assumed the music crowd would be the fastest and best source."

"The church crowd, too. Luke's big on that market. Or was."

"Someone else said that. But his band wasn't a religious group. I saw one of their demo videos. They weren't doing spirituals."

"Luke did any kind of stuff. He'd sing anywhere someone would let him, pay or not. Personally, I didn't think much of his voice."

"Why not?"

"Too perfect. A paint-by-numbers voice. A singer should have something different. My sister calls it punch."

"You ever hear Norman Blake sing 'Lorena'?"

"No."

"You know who Norman Blake is?"

"Doc Watson, Merle Watson, Tony Rice, Dan Crary."

"Okay. I didn't mean to challenge you."

"It's okay. I can't play a guitar, but I admire anyone who can, especially acoustic, flatpicking." The young man flipped one of the Daring Do cases, pointed at himself in the band photo. "I do harmony on this one."

Galway noted a small wound on the boy's hand, a ragged puncture between thumb and finger. He looked at the photo—three ladies and this young man, curly haired and muscular. Galway read the names. "You're Earl Wellington?"

"That's me."

"No instrument?"

"That's the problem. My sister's the real musician."

"At least you can sing."

The place suddenly burst into activity—a woman and a small, chubby boy came through the front door, just as a rapidly gesticulating student emerged from a back room, his guitar precariously held. Behind him came a frazzled looking instructor, who seemed concerned about the uncased guitar and who massaged the nape of his neck as though a headache was on its way. The phone rang, too. This was actually a business. Galway took out his wallet so he would be more than just a waiting question. When the boy handed him change and the sacked purchases, Galway asked, "Where's a good place for lunch?"

"Right next door. Bread and soup. Today it's black-bean soup and Russian rye."

"There it is!" The chubby boy pointed at something in the glass case. "An ocarina. Everybody in class is supposed to get one."

The boy's teacher, Galway mused, was dedicated or dangerous.

"That one's glazed clay, with twelve holes," Earl Wellington said, taking the item out and showing it to the boy, but handing it to the mother. "We have them in plastic."

"I want this one." The boy took it from his mother, but gently. "I don't want a plastic one." He put it toward his lips and the mother pushed it away. "Don't play it until we buy it."

Earl Wellington had placed a tiny box and three smaller ocarinas before them—blue, red, yellow, four holes each. He spoke now directly to the child, easily, buddy to buddy. "One of these you could stick in your pocket, and this," he opened the box and pulled out a bird-shaped ocarina strung on a thin leather strip, "you could wear around your neck. You could have it with you most of the time, if your mother said it was okay."

Galway hung around to see how the indecisive child would resolve his conflicting desires. Pangs of childhood. The boy ended up with the lovely bird piece around his neck and a blue plastic one in his hand. Indulgent and understanding mother. Thoughtful salesman.

At the recommended restaurant, Galway sat next to the window. Some of the younger customers dipped their bread in their soup, and he followed suit. A custom was a custom. He enjoyed the soup immensely, and the sunlight on the checkered tablecloth. A thin newspaper called *Blue River Review* had been left on the window sill, and he read it. It was largely ads and upcoming performances. He counted at least eighteen bands appearing the current month. He put the paper back on the ledge, went outside. He sat on a concrete tree well, inside it a straggling sapling. "Hang in there," he said.

He read the jewel-case inserts. They didn't include lyrics, just the names of musicians, title of songs, credits, and the production company. Some of the pieces were traditional, some original. Galway suspected the producers were the artists themselves, a common practice. The most common, probably, in the modern world.

He wondered why Earl hadn't asked who had been arrested. Maybe that had already hit the grapevine, too.

He called Andy. "Anything new?"

"Lab results are due anytime. What are you up to?"

"Learning about the victim's music."

"Funeral march."

"That's ugly, Andy."

"Sorry. You gave me an opening."

"Grave mistake." Galway hung up. Bad taste twice over.

* * *

Alone in the Musicians' Arte, Earl Wellington sat on the stool, the blue ocarina in his left hand. He stared at the floor, seeing in his mind's eye Johnny Rowland, who was a constant in the periphery of the music scene. He bought drinks for the musicians, called out for their favorite songs, gave them rides. Ran errands. Anyone could be pushed too far. Himself included. He raised his eyes to the sun-lighted street outside. This could be such a good life. It could be the best. But, damn it, it wasn't now and might not be ever again. He put the ocarina to his lips, covered the holes and played the part of "Elzic's Farewell" he had memorized. He stopped at the first flub. At this rate, he might be able to play the entire tune just before his own funeral.

* * *

Sheriff Bonnie and Walter were waiting. Galway shook hands with each, managing "Hey" and a smile that felt a little tight. He avoided meeting their eyes long, though the men had never been any less than friends. They were too concerned about his state of mind.

"Okay then," the sheriff said, moving on to business. He pushed the tape strip down enough for Galway and Walter to step over it, then followed them. "We're basically through here. The tape may come down tomorrow, so you're not asking too much. Anyone can come in after that. We've done a thorough job, too. All the same, Galway, don't mess up the scene. Walk right where I do or where I indicate, and don't touch anything. No photos. I wouldn't want us to lose a case because we acted out of turn here."

"You know, Bonnie, that I believe in full disclosure."

"No, I don't. I believe you keep your cards close to your chest till you know what's really at stake."

The sheriff was mid-forties, about ten years older than Galway, but they knew each other through family friendships. Bonnie's brother, Kyle, was Galway's age, a good friend, and was a sheriff of a Missouri Bootheel region, having married a girl from there. Bonnie was the name easily settled on from the original Boniface. His mother wasn't Catholic, but she loved the sound of the old name. Walter and Galway had been in the same class, gone to the same high school, and kept their friendship through college and afterward. They were still friends, though they didn't do much together anymore. Nothing at all for over a year.

"I also want to get reelected." Bonnie unlocked the front door to Michaels' house and entered first, holding the door for Galway and Walter. He was so muscular that his brown, sharply creased uniform strained at the seams, but he moved very gracefully. "Walter, you lead in, keep him on the right path."

Michaels hadn't been much into décor. Beneath the wide street-side window stretched a lime-green vinyl sofa. A nubby dark green blanket had been tucked in between the top and bottom cushions and drawn neatly tight. Adjacent at one end was an over-padded chair, upholstered in bristly blue and silver plaid. A black pole lamp stood at the other end of the sofa, its white top like an upside down bowl. Double lace curtains, incongruous with the other pieces, gave the illusion of openness, but really blocked anyone from seeing in or out. The grouping along the inner wall reflected the real center of interest. A huge keyboard was against the wall, above it a wall lamp, its plastic cord curling down like a gold vine. Beside the keyboard, a red guitar, so shiny it looked wet, rested in a chrome stand. On either side of the instruments, straight-backed kitchen chairs formed a semi-circle, the setting for jams.

Nothing really nice or attractive, but serviceable, and neat.

Galway stayed by the keyboard as Walter moved on. He had seen the guitar in the Fallen Angels video at Mrs. Dunbar's. A red plastic crate by the first chair held a number of large, spiral-bound books. Fake books.

He followed Walter into the next room, a kitchen. The cupboard doors were ajar, left that way by the officers, and there was little to see—a few colored plastic dishes and glasses. Luke's food stocks were canned goods, chili, soup, tuna, stew, spaghetti.

"Anything in the refrigerator?" Galway asked.

The chief slid a handkerchief through the handle, pulled it open.

The interior was neat and spare. Cheese, crackers, bread and bologna, milk, coffee and cola. "Not an epicurean," Galway said.

"Not a partier, either." From Walter. "Serious dude, I'd say."

The hallway floor was covered with a very lightweight, transparent plastic. Galway smelled something like bleach or a mineral. Heavy and acrid. Blood. "Is it my imagination, or do I smell blood?"

"It's not your imagination."

He had never smelled this particular odor. He clenched his lips, felt as if he might gag. He didn't want to breathe. He was momentarily lightheaded and looked back at the doorway. The other men were watching him, not unkindly.

"You okay?" from Bonnie.

"Yeah. Let's go on."

"Bathroom to your left," the chief said from behind, "and laundry room to your right. Bedrooms next. The one we want is on the right."

An attempt had been made to furnish the one to their left: an unfolded cot, two metal patio chairs, and an upended orange grate holding a tiny green lamp.

Walter stopped, turned to face Galway. "Here we are. Walk on the tape, not on the plastic. We sort of put it down with that in mind. Remember, don't touch anything."

The bedroom was fairly large for a small house, about twelve foot square. Here, too, the thin, clear plastic sheeting covered the floor. The furniture, surprisingly, was a matched walnut set. The door opened on the far right of the room. Clockwise from the door, ceiling-high bookcases jutted out enough to conceal what came next, a closet door, then a narrow door to the exterior, a folding chair that obviously served as bed-stand, holding a tall, narrow lamp, the bed, stripped to old mattress. On the north wall, another dresser, wider, with an attached oval mirror, tilted down. Then a window with green curtains. Green was the prevailing color scheme, Galway thought. An attempt at style with little money to spare and not much interest.

Galway walked forward to see the space between bed and dresser. Through the plastic a black stain was visible, disappearing under the bed. Johnny should have noticed the smell. How could he not have?

"Well, there was lots of blood," Galway said. "The murderer couldn't have come out clean."

"He wasn't clean. He had blood on his shoes."

Along with the nausea, he felt heavy and tired. He wanted Johnny to be truthful, worth everyone's concern. Of course, any human was *worth* concern. What he meant was *worthy*. He wanted Johnny to be a worthy person, because his aunt believed he was.

Galway indicated the door next to the mirror-dresser. "Was that used or do you know?"

"The door's bolted shut, top, bottom and midway," Bonnie said, "and hasn't been opened for a long time. The guy came through the laundry room window." He opened a closet door. "This is where he kept his normal clothes."

The clothing was arranged by kind, shirts together, slacks together, sweatshirts folded on shelves, shoes side by side.

"Spartan fellow," Galway said.

"It's easy to be organized," Walter said, "if you don't have much."

Galway looked around the room again. The wooden floors appeared worn. The furniture too, heavy and dark. There were no rugs anywhere in the room, even by the bed. He squatted, peering through the plastic at the floor, and knelt more to look under the bed.

"What are you looking for?" from the sheriff.

"Trying to see something no one else noticed. It could happen." Galway said. He had seen scratches on the floor by the dresser and wanted to look closer. Instead, he stood. "Did your guys remove anything?"

"Like what?"

"Rugs, towels, a weapon?"

"Nope. A body and what was in his pockets."

While he followed them, careful to step only on the tape, Galway scanned the contents of the bookcase. Nothing religious, not even a Bible. A biography of Jim Morrison. A few magazines and catalogs, a photo-book on the making of *The Last Waltz*, stacks of what appeared to be song collections, more fake books— and two rows of black-spined leather volumes. Now this was different. They didn't fit with the rest of the house. Journals?

"Here's his professional attire," Walter said. "I think that's what these are." He stood by a now open closet.

Luke had a few costumes different only in color. Boots. Black, brown, and white leather jackets held together with a few strategic strips, so they appeared mostly fringe and seams. The pants, too, same varied colors, were long leather strips between top thigh and ankle, as if standard pant legs had been cut vertically to appear whole until the wearer moved quickly, gyrated to music. Then the outfit would suggest slashed flesh. This Galway had seen in action, as had Mrs. Dunbar. Under colored strobe lights, it would be even more suggestive.

"He was very neat," Galway said. "It's pretty boring overall, though. Dry. Seems in contrast with his interest in music. Was he into drugs?"

"We didn't find anything," from the sheriff.

"It's odd. There's no pleasure in this place."

"Music."

"Maybe. Maybe even that wasn't really pleasant for him."

Outside the yellow tape again, the sheriff asked, "Well, Galway, did you see something we should know about?"

"No. I'd need a closer look."

"That's as close as you get for now. It's a look-close by the book. The best we can do."

"I appreciate it, too."

"Got a little sick, didn't you?"

"A little."

"After the first time, it doesn't hit you as much, but it's still pretty powerful."

They hung around a few minutes. The sheriff talked about a training video for new officers, a real tape from a policeman's car. He stopped right in the middle of the story, said, "We need to get back." Walter offered his hand to Galway, gripped Galway's briefly. "Let's do something soon, all right? I know—I'll teach you how to fish. I'll even clean the damned things for you. That's if you can catch anything."

"I'll do it," Galway said. "Soon as this is over."

He felt them looking at him as they drove away. He waved. Walter's arm shot out the passenger window, waving in return.

The two men in the car smiled at each other. "We're going to get him back."

"Maybe. Even if we do, he's not ever going to be the same."

"Well, you know, who is? If you lose your parents, part of your life is irretrievable," Walter said. "You're the adult. You can't run home to Mom and Pop."

"It hit him harder for some reason. It changed him."

"We're going to get him back, I tell you." He slapped the dashboard. "Just watch."

"He never was a fisherman, so don't set your heart on that."

"Let's get him smoking again."

Silence.

"Do you think he's gay?" from Boniface.

"I've wondered."

"That could be why he can't rally. Because he never told them."

"Or because he did."

Galway stayed on the sidewalk, feeling as if the noxious odor from inside was still in his lungs. Alone, he spit a couple of times and he allowed himself a few deep, deep breaths, exhaling each fully. Then he brought himself to the task—the books inside. They had to be journals. They weren't all the same size, though they at first appeared to be. He wanted to get back in the house, just for a few minutes. Steal a look at a book or two. "Steal Away." That had been one of the choir songs.

From the corner house came a familiar voice.

"How'd you get them to take you inside?"

"I may wind up doing the cleanup," Galway said. It wasn't really a lie. For all he now knew, that work could fall to him. Though, admittedly, it wasn't likely. "Did you remember anything about a car?"

"I did think about that. He had two. A green one and a yellow one."

"He owned two cars?"

"Maybe. They were never parked here at the same time."

"What makes?"

"Why?"

Galway couldn't come up with a reason. "I don't know. It's interesting, I guess, and those guys would like to know. You could tell them."

"You tell them for me," Mr. Welker said.

"Okay," Galway said. "It'll give me a chance to follow up on the work here."

"Do you remove trees?"

"I haven't yet. I might be able to. I don't see why not."

"It's not a big one. I don't mind you leaving the roots, either. Just get it down under the ground level. That's it there."

"It's a thorn tree."

"Yeah. I'd like a friendlier tree. Maybe a pecan, or a plum. Something I might work with. Maybe even get a bag or two of fruit to give away. Given, that is, that I live long enough for it to come to fruition. You get that? Fruition?"

"I got it. Nice. And you'll make that easily. We'll get one big enough that it'll bear at least the second year."

"Good. I can make it that long. Maybe even three or more."

Removing a thorn tree wasn't appealing; helping a ninety-year-old man was. The tree wasn't thriving anyway. It was fairly bedraggled, old and partly dead, partly well-leafed. A thin, broken lower branch dangled like a small number seven. He pointed at the raw break. "How did that happen?"

"I don't know. Just noticed it myself."

Galway walked to his truck. He had to talk to Johnny again. How could the kid have not seen the body and yet have tracked blood to the window?

Galway filled a few hours with work he had agreed to do. He mowed a large, sloping, empty lot behind a house down the street. With the mower silent, he put his portable CD player nearby and played the new CDs while he worked, tuning in occasionally, other times attending only the pleasant, cleansing physical labor. He bagged the cuttings, raked and bagged rotten apples that smelled so strongly he felt slightly drunk. Two houses up, again to the background of music, he loaded four railroad ties that had formed a garden, now overgrown. He shoveled out weeds, digging down for the roots. He raked the ground smooth.

He was paid in cash by one woman, with check by the other. Each of them had inspected his work, a process that always made him nervous. He expected complaints because he always saw what remained—a straggly weed, a stick, a crooked brick, a bush turning brown from outside in.

Each had been pleased.

Heading home, he turned on the portable player and then, in his garage, stayed in the truck, continuing to listen to the CDs. He realized that the music he had noticed while working was by the Daring Do. He had tuned out much—not all—but much of Luke Michaels' Fallen Angels. He did like the Angels' "Turn Around Time." The chorus, fragmented, staccato words echoed in sharp bell tones, were, when understood together, totally sensical: "*let's crash the century/knot up father time/slice the rainbow into ribbons/make the devil dance in time.*" Jumbled as they were on the CD, sometimes the phrase was "*devil time,*" "*time dance,*" "*slice father,*" "*ribbon time,*" and other pairs. The music was really catchy, and the rhythm, but the words were somewhat ugly.

Inside the house, a message from Andy awaited him. "Call me. It's not what I expected, for sure."

Luke Michaels had been stabbed four times. The last wound had been inflicted with a different weapon, with far more force, and upward.

"It was a type of dagger," Andy said, "sharp on both sides. Whoever wielded this one meant to kill Luke. And did. Get this—it may have been inflicted an hour or so after the others. The scenario changes, huh? "

"Yeah, it does," Galway said. "It suggests two attackers."

"Maybe. Maybe Johnny just made sure before he left the house."

In spite of Andy's last words, Galway found the new information hopeful. It didn't actually make a case for Johnny's innocence. He could have been the attacker both times. Or he could have been the first attacker, or the last. But it did make the case more complex and the answers equally so. Johnny didn't appear to be passionate or angry or devious. He was less likely to be the mastermind, so to speak, if the case weren't a simple burglary interrupted.

After a quick meal of hotdogs and pork-and-beans, which would have made Andy groan in disgust, Galway strolled over to Mrs. Dunbar's. He rattled the screen door. "News," he called.

"It's open."

She was at the kitchen counter, in one of her work outfits, light brown slacks and long-sleeved blue shirt, her forearms resting on the edge of the sink. The posture emphasized the unnatural curve of her back. Galway realized that raising her arms even slightly, as she was now doing, was probably difficult and uncomfortable. She was applying toothpaste, it appeared, to a necklace.

"I guess there's a reason for that," he said.

"Toothpaste is a good metal polish, particularly for silver. You said news?"

"Yeah, and I think it's good news."

She rinsed the necklace and her hands, dried both with a soft flannel rag, and led him into the living room.

He repeated Andy's report, including Andy's statement that Johnny could have delivered the fatal blow as well as the others.

"If I don't believe Johnny would stab a man capable of defending himself, I'm certainly not going to believe he would stab one already fallen. He's not a coward. He was a sturdy little fellow and brave in his own way."

"I just want you to be prepared. If someone came in after Johnny, maybe that person dealt the final blow. But if Johnny was there last . . ."

"First, second, or last, he's not a killer, Galway. He might defend himself. "

"Or someone else?"

"Yes. He's not a bad kid."

"I don't think he is, either. Listen, Mrs. Dunbar, did you already return the videos to the church?"

"Yes. I said I'd get them right back, and that's exactly what I did. Why?"

"I'd like to listen to them again, at least the one of Luke's band. I was listening to his CDs today and realized I hadn't paid attention to the music itself."

"Why would that be important?"

"I'm not sure. But I want to hear the songs again."

"Father Madison didn't really want me to take them the first time. You could just go by there, and play them on the spot."

"I'm not fond of churches, Mrs. Dunbar, and am especially not fond of priests."

"I'm not fond of asking for things when the person doesn't want to give them to me."

Her sincerity persuaded him. Asking was something she found distasteful. "Okay. I'll run by there."

"No. I've changed my mind. I'll do it. This was my idea and it's my job."

"Are you sure?"

"Yes. It's for my nephew, after all. I don't mind. I'll get the videos in the morning."

"Thanks. I'll visit Johnny again, see if he can fill in some gaps."

Before he left, she cleaned his watchband. "You can't use just any toothpaste," she said. "Some kinds are too abrasive."

"That reminds me, I was breathing old blood all afternoon." He waited for some kind of response.

"It won't hurt you," she said, "but you might rinse your mouth out with a little salt water or hydrogen peroxide. Not both, though."

At home, he cleansed his mouth with the milder, more familiar treatment, salt water. Then he got the small box holding his father's cufflinks, a tube of toothpaste, and a box of tissues. At first he listened to the Fallen Angels CD while he polished the cufflinks, but soon he turned off the CD, put on an album. His mother had liked tenor voices. His father probably had one, though he couldn't recall him singing a complete tune. He was a hummer. A humming tenor.

> *Thou will come no more, Gentle Annie,*
> *Like a flow'r, thy spirit did depart,*
> *Thou art gone, alas! like the many,*
> *That have bloomed in the summer of my heart.*

~5~

Magic or Meanness

FRIDAY MORNING, GALWAY SAT ACROSS FROM JOHNNY IN THE
common visiting room.

"Yeah," Johnny said, "I knew something was wrong. I could feel
it, you know? I mean, the minute I got in the house. A chill.
Real spooky."

"Why didn't you leave immediately?"

"I didn't get real scared then. I mean I was *sort* of scared the
whole time, but I didn't know I was spooked till later. Then I
remembered that I'd known something was wrong the minute I
got inside. I guess it was the smell."

"Hard to miss even now. Must have been terrible."

"I don't know. I don't remember it that way."

"The body was hard to miss, too."

"I swear I didn't see a body."

"But you *did* go into the bedroom? All the way in?"

"Maybe to the foot of the bed."

"Maybe?" Galway said, exasperated with what was beginning to
look like evasion and not just imprecision. "Apply yourself, fellow,
okay? This is important. Tell me exactly what happened, the
truth. Don't shift it around to explain new evidence or evidence
that might turn up later. What you did is what you did. Period."

"I really don't remember exactly. Something was wrong. I mean,
I was in the bedroom, sort of, barely, but something was wrong.
That's what I remember. I think I froze for a few minutes. Then I
got out of there as fast as I could."

"You weren't so afraid that you left the equipment behind. And
you hung around."

"I wanted to throw the stuff back in the window. I hadn't stolen anything before, nothing big, I mean, and something was weird. But then I figured I could get caught just the same. I'd already *been* in there. It was done. That's breaking and entering. Well, entering, I guess. I didn't break anything to enter."

The kid couldn't be guilty of much. If he were, he was a great dissembler. "Did you take anything besides recording equipment?"

"Nope. He didn't have anything else."

"A book?"

"Why would anybody take a book?"

He was truly perplexed and Galway was somewhat thankful. The puzzlement fit with Johnny's general naiveté.

"Okay, Johnny. How could you have gotten blood on your shoes if you didn't get near the body?"

"I don't know. I swear. Maybe it was somewhere else in the house. Maybe it was outside. I don't know where it came from. Maybe somebody *put* it on my shoe." He glanced up at the video camera, then back to Galway. "Was Luke under the bed?"

"I don't know where he was when you were in his house."

"Where does the report say they found my footprints? I mean shoeprints?"

"Hallway and window. They're checking your car. I suspect they'll find blood there, too."

The boy had blanched and now chewed down on the cigarette filter.

Galway remained quiet a few seconds, though it seemed much longer, watching Johnny and giving him a chance to come forth with anything he was holding back. Then he moved into rougher ground. "Did Mr. Fielding tell you about the autopsy report?"

Johnny shook his head quickly, his expression reflecting interest and fear. But who, Galway admitted, wouldn't be frightened in this situation?

"He was stabbed four times. Above the heart, in the throat, and twice in the abdomen. One abdominal wound differs from the others."

Johnny seemed to be holding his breath. When Galway didn't continue, Johnny asked, "Differs how?"

"It was deeper, inflicted later, and with a different knife. It's the wound that killed him."

Johnny had paled so much that Galway thought the boy might faint. He was unsteady, as if he felt a distant quake.

"I didn't do it."

"Did you help someone else do it?"

No response. Galway had apparently become for Johnny a source of possible harm. Johnny was retreating into wherever Johnny retreated.

"He may have been in a struggle, Johnny. Someone may have held him while someone else stabbed him. Maybe you only came along with a friend, but things got out of control?"

When the silence continued, Galway spoke gently. "Okay. Ease up. Even if you won't defend yourself, your aunt will. Luke is dead and somebody killed him. If we're going to get you out of trouble then we have to figure out who did." That was apparently a welcome statement, but not enough to free the stranglehold of Johnny's fear. "Maybe someone had a grudge." Galway waited a few seconds more. "Try to calm down a little, okay? You've got help."

Just as he lowered the receiver, he heard a faint "hey" and brought it back up.

"Thanks," Johnny said, though he was looking at the guard who had started to enter the room and was now withdrawing, "for the cigarettes. I'll pay you back."

"You don't have to. Just don't tell your aunt."

"Listen, could . . . could you get it in the paper that I didn't see the murderer? I'm afraid the guy will kill me, too," Johnny said, "if he thinks I saw him."

The statement was a sure sign of innocence, unless Johnny had said it for exactly that reason. "The sheriff's people and the prosecutor think *you* did it," Galway said. "That's our first concern." He stressed *our.*

The guard opened the door again.

"How do they do that?" Johnny said. "If they're not listening in, how do they know we're through?"

"Experience. The guard's watching us on the monitor and reads body language."

As if cued, the guard pulled back.

Johnny looked at the corner across from him, where a camera

angled down. "They can probably read lips."

Galway thought maybe they could, but he wasn't going to say so. "As long as you're feeling better, let me ask you about something else. You know anything about Luke's car?"

"He had a nice one sometimes. I don't know if it was his. An old Ford, in good condition. It was a Ford Fairlane, 1960s. He didn't take care of it. Somebody probably stole it, too. The same guy. Am I going to get blamed for that?"

"No one's mentioned it yet."

"Well, don't bring it up."

"Okay," Galway smiled. "I won't. But you can bet, Johnny, that someone will. Or has. Did he have two cars?"

"Sometimes he didn't have any. He hitched rides a lot and took taxis. But I know what you're talking about. He drove a green Dodge every now and then, a little hatchback model. It had a dented right rear door, right?"

"I don't know. I haven't seen it."

"It was probably a loaner when the Ford was out."

"Out with whom?"

"One of his girls."

Again that odd tone, a little pained, bitter.

"Which girl, Johnny?"

Johnny shrugged. "Any of them. They all liked him."

They hung up. Galway was reaching for the doorknob on his side when he heard a dull thunking, and looked back. Johnny had obviously knocked on the glass. Galway went back, lifted the phone.

"I remember," Johnny said, "that the Ford was a gift to Luke. He didn't have any money and suddenly he popped up with this car. He said it was a present, a birthday present. He didn't tell me specifically, but I heard him say it."

"Good job. That'll help. Any more?"

"Nobody ever gave *me* a car." Johnny held the receiver up and spoke to the camera. "We're done here, thank you."

He had aligned himself with the man leaving, with Galway. Not so slow, this kid, Galway thought.

* * *

68

Mrs. Dunbar had picked up the videos only to discover, at home, that one was missing—the Fallen Angels video. She called Rosie, who said she had simply given Mrs. Dunbar the same stack as before. If any were missing, she wasn't aware of it, and she couldn't check with Father Madison because he wouldn't be back to the parish house until later in the day, probably evening when the Vestry met.

No way to complete the task.

Mrs. Dunbar drove to talk with Zeena about Johnny. Generally it was best to stay out of another's business but sometimes a person should speak up. Parents shouldn't abandon children without great cause, and maybe not even then. Own them, and all their sorrows and evils. Claiming the person wasn't the same as claiming the wrong he might have done, just him, the human.

She couldn't understand why Johnny would steal, unless it was for attention. Was he in need? true need? That would be a shame for the whole family—for herself, too. She should have known and helped.

Maybe she was just curious and invasive, and wanted to be where the action was. Not action, really. Just life. Being lived and not observed.

Zeena was home alone. Her eyes glistened. She looked like a person who had been stopped in the course of fleeing. Mrs. Dunbar had the urge to calm her as she would a frightened animal. "If it's a bad time," Mrs. Dunbar said softly, "I don't need to stay. I can come by later."

"No, no, that's fine." Zeena's arms were crossed tightly, as if she shielded naked breasts.

"Are you certain? I smell something baking. I don't want to be a bother."

"No. You're not a bother. I'm finished in the kitchen and I . . . welcome the company. I've been trying to stay busy so I won't worry. I want to keep a positive attitude. That's so important, Letitia. If I can keep positive thoughts, white, you know? Thinking pure? But if I think about Johnny or what he may have done or what may happen to him, I get ill. I don't *want* that to happen, but it does. I'm afraid I could make something happen just by thinking on it too much. I might focus a bad energy and draw it to us."

Mrs. Dunbar enjoyed colorful people, and she didn't condemn beliefs different from her own, but she didn't want to entertain certain thoughts, and the concept Zeena had expressed, "white" thoughts, wasn't totally unfamiliar to Mrs. Dunbar. It often had to do with witchcraft, with blocking access to one's mind and energies. Some subjects a wise person avoided thinking about too much, but should let them stay unfamiliar, even a little frightening. Zeena's statement, though, was similar to saying "think on all things good and holy" in biblical terms, she supposed. And not her business in any case. Not really. Letitia focused on Zeena, who was obviously struggling emotionally. "You have a sensitive constitution. You don't have to apologize for it."

"Yes, I do. Peter thinks I'm on the fringe of frantic, or maybe it's frenetic. Whatever. He says I stir myself up and make everyone else pay for it."

"We all have natures we were born with, and some are more troublesome than others. That goes for Johnny, too. Could we talk about him? I wonder why he would. . ."

"I'm redoing his room," Zeena said. "Come see." She headed for the stairs, talking rapidly. "It's not really his room, since he doesn't live here now, but it's still connected to him, right? I mean, my touch in the room might reach Johnny somehow, right? Now it's a place of healing. That has to be a good thing."

Mrs. Dunbar, a few steps behind Zeena, recognized another attempt to have an effect from a distance. "It might," she offered. "Who knows? Maybe even good thoughts travel to the right place."

Zeena turned at the top of the stairs. "Exactly," she said. "I know that happens, even when people don't want it to. Thoughts have real presence. Power. You can channel them. You can send them. Just like prayers, only from you to someone else."

Mrs. Dunbar wanted the communication between them to continue, but the subject quickened her heartbeat. Zeena was talking witchcraft, no matter how she sought to call it something else. Mrs. Dunbar took a deep breath and attacked the last steps. One result of a bent spine was difficulty breathing. The lungs couldn't expand properly.

Zeena had re-wallpapered the room. It was a pale blue paper, with a pattern that Mrs. Dunbar finally managed to decipher: bird cages, with doors open. Every bird had apparently flown the coop and was disappearing into the blue background, the distant forms looking like tiny, widespread wings.

"Blue is a peaceful color," Zeena said. "It eases the spirit."

"I'm fond of blue myself."

Zeena half-raised her arms, hands palm up and out, a simple gesture of welcome. "I've tried to bring the sky in here."

"I see that." Mrs. Dunbar tried to ease toward the subject she wanted to broach. "I imagine Johnny longs to be here right now. He was worried about you when he called me."

Zeena stilled herself, facing Mrs. Dunbar. "I can't handle him, Letitia. I haven't been able to since he was fourteen. If he's here, I have to take medication. I'm angry all the time and want to jerk him up and yell at him and kick his lazy ass out the door. I can't bear even to talk about him. I can't fix him so I don't want him around."

"I know you've had a hard time with him, but you need to know he was concerned for *you*. He wanted me to break the news to you and Peter because he couldn't risk having you answer the phone. He loves you, Zeena. He wants you to love him."

"I do! I do! But I don't like him. I'm sick of him. That's terrible, isn't it? Oh, I know it is, and I'm sorry about it, but it's the way things are. It's his fault as much as ours. Mine."

"Maybe you could write him. Or visit him. Just visit him. This Saturday you could. . ."

"I'm not going out to the jail, Letitia. If I have to visit my son in jail, then I'll never see him again."

It was pain speaking, Mrs. Dunbar knew. The words didn't matter. That was anguish. Zeena both loved and hated her own child, and didn't know if that conflict rose from his nature or her own. She was trapped. "It's all right," Mrs. Dunbar said. "I agree that it's probably not a good idea to visit him."

"I don't know anything about what happened and don't want to."

"Did he need money, Zeena? You can tell me that. Why would he steal? You and Peter have enough to help the boy."

Zeena bent to tug wrinkles, invisible to Mrs. Dunbar, from the bedspread. When she raised up, she repositioned the bed lamp. With a final glance as if to insure that everything was perfect, she walked toward the doorway. "I shouldn't have said what I did in this room. Let's go on the patio."

"It'll be good for both of us." Mrs. Dunbar followed her down the stairs. "I've been too judgmental and have you on the defensive when you have enough stress. Let's just calm down together. How's that?"

"I *do* love Johnny," Zeena said.

"I don't doubt it at all."

Zeena stopped at the stove to put on the kettle. Mrs. Dunbar went on outside to allow Zeena time to compose herself, or even just to disappear if that's what she wanted. Who was she, Mrs. Dunbar, to decide what another woman could and could not bear?

It was a carefully tended yard. The flower beds were randomly placed, and randomly seeded, with a resulting explosive mixture of colors and blooms, many violets, geranium, bluebells, indigo, phlox, day lilies, columbine, blazing star. Morning glories on trellises. All this was Peter's handiwork. Herbs grew among the more common flowers, in narrow beds along the fence, and in huge clay pots. Zeena's touch. Two visible, vying philosophies.

Zeena emerged, carrying a tray which rattled as she lowered it to the patio table. "Peter had offered, *we* had offered, to buy a small house for Johnny near the university, if Johnny would enroll. He could take in a roommate or two and feel independent. We'd pay all his expenses. But he doesn't want to go to college."

"Maybe he's just not ready and knows it."

"He doesn't have any pride, Letitia, not for himself. And no respect for us, not even for Peter, who would do anything for him. He wants to dress in those bummy clothes, wear his hair like a clown, and be free in the evening to stay at bars until midnight. He chain smokes. I'm not even sure he inhales, but he keeps one going all the time. We make him go outside, but when we're not here, he lights anywhere and then sprays something and thinks that covers it. Or that's what he *was* doing. We told him he follows the rules or he's out. So he moved in with a taxi driver and now he wants to be a taxi mechanic. He's been helping out there for free. He's a loser, Letitia. He has a follower's mind. Give him a master and he'll grovel.

But he won't respect me or his father."

"That doesn't make him a murderer, though."

"Don't say that word. I hate to think of it. I hate to think of it." She rolled her eyes. "I don't want to think we caused this."

"Of course you didn't cause it. And don't believe for a minute, Zeena, that he killed anybody. I don't believe it. But you need to know the situation. Johnny was definitely in the house. And there was blood on his shoes."

Zeena covered her face with her hands, but only briefly. "What am I supposed to do? Keep suffering because of him?"

"I have an attorney friend who's working for Johnny, and who found someone to represent him. Whatever you tell me, I'll tell them. If they need to see you, I'll come with them. If you *want* me to. Only then. I'll be a buffer if I can. You just tell me what you need. Right now, though, can you tell me why he would steal? Does he have any need to steal? anything . . . special he wants?"

"You mean is he on drugs. No I don't think so. Peter doesn't think so, either. Johnny's a little afraid of medications. But cigarettes he's crazy for. I don't think he drinks much either, not really. . . He should be okay as far as money goes. He's supposed to pay for his car insurance, but we probably pay that and no telling what else. I'm sure Peter gives him a hundred a week, and I suspect he gives him more whenever Johnny drops by the store. Sometimes Johnny will do inventory or stocking. Especially if he needs cigarettes. We think he gives money away. He thinks that's being a big man and being a friend. He's just a donor for bums."

"It isn't a totally bad trait."

"It is if the money comes from someone else."

"That does change the nature of generosity, doesn't it? He hasn't stolen before?"

Zeena shook her head. "Not that we know of. His trouble has always been going along with the guys. A bunch of them spent the night in a vacant house over on Leicester, and then they broke out all the windows. Someone called the police, and everyone but Johnny ran home. He stayed and talked to the officers. They didn't arrest him, but they could have. He's foolish, Letitia, absolutely. He'll do anything somebody suggests. Set off a fire alarm, cut down a hedge, drink rubbing alcohol."

"Did he really do that? Drink rubbing alcohol?"

"Someone told him it was safe. He mixed it with something, probably orange juice. He likes orange juice. He wound up in the emergency room and asked the clerk to call us. He was really sick. It burned his throat, tore up his stomach. But I'm glad it happened. The one thing he's really afraid of is getting sick. He'll drop by when he's not feeling well. He slept in the porch swing one night. I saw him. He left a couple cigarette butts behind the rose bush." Zeena stood up. "I have to get my mind off him, Letitia. My heart's still racing. I'm so angry. I need to get busy."

"I didn't mean to make you ill. I just want to help him."

"It's all right. Sometimes I can't help running away. It just happens. I feel I'll die if I have to stay still and listen."

"You'll be fine, Zeena. You *are* fine. I think you're sad more than angry." Mrs. Dunbar picked up her purse. "Maybe you would enjoy a more strenuous activity."

"You mean work it off? That's what Peter says. But it's not enough for me. I enjoy research and I love computer work. It's fast. I can go fifteen places in seconds. On the inside, I mean. A hundred."

They took the brick pathway around the house. Mrs. Dunbar admired, as she always did, the narrow, graceful windows that would catch the morning light. The sills were eye level and a sliver of blue on the nearest one caused her to glance at the other window. Just where the white paint of the siding met the painted window frame, was a slim line of blue. It wouldn't be noticeable from a distance and even up close was more like a shadow than a color. The sight tugged at Mrs. Dunbar's memory—blue at a portal. What did it mean, what did it mean? She recalled just as they reached her car. It kept evil spirits from entering. The house had snippets of magic everywhere. Zeena was protecting her life in her own way.

Mrs. Dunbar hesitated to hug Zeena, but sensing that Zeena was waiting for exactly that gesture, warmly embraced her. "You might feel better if you didn't read about home remedies and witchcraft and religions. Some subjects are more unsettling than others."

"They're interesting, though, Letitia. I'm not a soap-opera

woman. It's history, you know? Women herbalists were the first doctors, the first real ones. It was a woman who created digitalis, though a male took the long-term credit. They called what she had made a 'concoction.'"

"It's good to know facts like that, but if you dwell too much on injustices, you make yourself miserable and you can even stymie yourself. You can't be as effective helping people if you're overwrought all the time. Anger has its powers, but constant anger can hurt you. Even kill you."

"Peter calls that being 'fired up.' That's how it feels, too." She chuckled softly. "Fire me up and get out of the way. You know, maybe you and Peter think I should train for a marathon."

"Not if you didn't want to. We neither of us would wish you to be unhappy."

"I could run right now, five, ten miles."

"One or two would be a good start."

"I may do that. I'll leave Peter a note and say I'm out running around."

Mrs. Dunbar was relieved to hear the chuckle, a very nice sound, healthy and normal. Well, maybe it was *all* normal. A chuckle at the wrong time could, she supposed, be very unhealthy. The balance again—one action, two interpretations.

At the library, Mrs. Dunbar leafed through numerous books on herbal remedies before selecting three that seemed most detailed, accessible, and not repetitious. Then she moved to the section of books on magic. Even being there seemed wrong, which, she knew, was ridiculous. It sprang from her upbringing and the warning not to invite certain knowledge or experience. That was opening a portal to the unknown. But Zeena's activities had piqued her interest and it was hard not to satisfy curiosity. Maybe she would understand Zeena better.

Mrs. Dunbar remained standing to examine the witchcraft books, and finally chose three. She put them on top of the others to carry them. In her car, though, she said "For Pete's sake, Letitia," and placed her hand flat on each book. "See? They're harmless." Then she rearranged the small stack, forcing herself to treat the books like simple paper, powerless unless she made them otherwise. She rolled down the car window, took a deep breath.

"That's better," she said. Admittedly, she was wary of the old texts in a confined space, as if they gave off a force, not just a musty odor.

At home, she donned a robe, then took a nap so she would be fresh enough to drive to the church in late day traffic. She still had to acquire that missing video.

* * *

Mrs. Dunbar arrived at the parish house a few minutes after 5:00, to find that Rosie was gone for the day and the Vestry meeting was already in progress. She could hear voices from the corner room down the hall. Ill at ease in Rosie's office, where the empty desk and electronic equipment seemed foreign and too still for night hours, she went down the hall to the library. The muted voices made her feel more at ease, one person among many. She crossed the library in semi dark, turned on a table lamp and sat down in a deep, comfortable chair. Across from her, thick volumes lined a shelf. In a moment, she realized what they were—photo albums, a visual record of church social activities.

They were in chronological order, with major events noted in a front panel. She looked for ones from two years ago, when Luke first came to the church, and carried them back to her chair, stacked them on the floor at her feet. She leafed through the plastic pages. Each held six or more photos, but she could scan them quickly. Many of events she remembered well, some she had not attended, but the photos highlighted people and details she would probably never have noted on the day itself. The photographer took mostly complimentary shots. Betty Miles, for example, was usually the focus of any male talking with her, even if his wife was also in the picture. And Betty always had a friendly expression.

In the third volume, Mrs. Dunbar encountered a few photos of Luke Michaels. She somberly considered only him in each photo— his eyes, wide brow, thick hair, the set of mouth. She traced the image with fingertip, reminding herself he was lost to the world now, which was sad. He was a young person—or had been—and now his choices were gone with him. Then she reexamined each photo for the total context, other people, setting, and again Luke. Luke with the choir, then at a church picnic, then at a lawn gathering. At the latter, he was obviously with Anne Mercer, the young front-row choir member. Mrs. Dunbar turned back a few pages, looked for Anne specifically. In two shots, she was with someone else, the tall, black-haired Leroy Atkins. So they had perhaps been more than fellow choir members. She noticed something else she had missed the first time through. Off to the side, seated on the same retaining wall as the couple, was Johnny. He had attended the social. Mrs. Dunbar remembered that. She had encouraged him to come, to meet some nice young people. And there he was. Sweet, hungry young fellow, eating ice cream, but looking at Anne.

She had to force her mind away from speculation about Johnny, and reviewed the photos again.

Yes, Anne and Leroy had been friends, at least, and Mrs. Dunbar suspected more. And obviously Luke had become Anne's focus, or was at a later gathering. They were standing on the sidewalk before the church. Anne, tall and slender, was standing a bit slouched, as if to appear shorter. She looked happy and hopeful, her dark eyes on her blonde companion. Luke didn't appear so taken with Anne. The photo held Mrs. Dunbar's attention, and she finally decided it was the perfect balance of the photo. The church in the background, arched doors wide open, a few people descending on each side of the broad steps, and the couple in the foreground. Light and darkness, interior and exterior, group and individual.

Mrs. Dunbar closed the album. A person could always find something that seemed significant, whether or not it actually was. Human beings interpreted reality and sometimes recast it. Some were more driven than others to change their lot. She returned the albums to the shelf, then, hesitantly, took one down again, flipping to the ice cream social and a photo of herself. It was most flattering. She wanted to slip it from the album simply to have a copy made. Surely it was the height of vanity to be investigating a murder, and become sidetracked with one's own image.

The sound of a door opening and men's voices alerted her that the Vestry meeting had recessed or ended, and she stepped into the hallway. Only Father Madison had left the group. The other men were still around the table in the room behind him.

"Letitia," Father Madison said. "How can I help you?"

"I didn't want to interrupt you," Mrs. Dunbar said. "But Rosie didn't give me one of the videos. The one of Luke Michaels' band. The label said 'Fallen Angels.'"

"Oh, that. It's in my office." His words were clipped. He leaned toward the meeting room. "One of you come get me when you're ready." Then he led Mrs. Dunbar to his office. "I planned to give the tape to the Michaels' family today," he said, opening the door, "but there was no opportunity."

"Are they here? In town?"

He shook his head. "No, they aren't. And they won't be." An open briefcase was on his desk. He took a tape from it. "It's really sad. A young man like that and no one really grieving."

Mrs. Dunbar felt guilty immediately. Luke Michaels was, after all—or had been—a living young man with mother, father, sister, brother. Surely. He couldn't have been totally alone. "It *is* sad," she said. "But maybe a name or phone number will turn up. He had friends."

"Don't worry about it, Letitia. Your own family has enough right now."

From the doorway came a man's voice. "Father Madison, if you think the church can afford to cushion all the pews *and* give you a raise, then why can't we buy one truly silver chalice instead of just *dipping* everything."

"You're not serious," the rector said.

"In a way I am."

"He's joking," Mrs. Dunbar said.

"Ha!" from Phil. "Letitia got it."

The rector still looked puzzled.

"Baptism," Mrs. Dunbar explained. She looked at Phil. "Actually the pun doesn't work, because Episcopalian's don't *dip*, they sprinkle. Dipping would be immersion."

"I wasn't being that serious." Phil went down the hall.

"I still don't get it," Father Madison said.

"It wasn't funny anyhow," she said. "What he really wants is for our communion serving ware to be all silver and not silver plated."

The rector wasn't one for humor or banter or even innuendoes. His strengths lay elsewhere. He was a thoughtful, direct, and sweet man, who loved the beauty in the world.

6

A Wealth of Words

GALWAY, AFTER TALKING WITH JOHNNY FRIDAY MORNING, HAD gone to Andy's office, to meet with the other members of the Fallen Angels band.

Sitting in deep leather chairs before Andy's desk, the two looked as if they were into long-distance running or into heavy dieting. Each was about six feet tall, 150 lbs., with jet-black hair, now tied back, to his waist. Each was dressed in jeans, work-boots, and a short-sleeved, plaid shirt. Each was also pleasant and courteous. Hank and Merle. Brothers. Galway had seen them recently, attired in leather pants and vests. Here, now, they were as wholesome as wheat.

"We had an act," Merle said, "and Luke joined us. Then he sort of became the lead. It was okay with us."

"Yeah. We're not too ambitious."

"We're trying to buy a garage."

"Merle's a good mechanic."

"We both are."

"You're mechanics?"

"Off and on."

"Do you know anything about Michaels' cars? We know he had two, one a collectable. Neither has shown up."

"He probably sold it. He was trying to. He wanted a lot of money for it, though, or we would have taken it."

"I offered him eight thousand on a time-payment deal, but he wanted more and all at once. He planned to buy some studio time, make a demo DVD."

"Do you know who might have wanted to kill him?"

"Me." That was from Merle.

"Don't joke around," from his brother. "You want to get us both thrown in jail?"

"Why?" Galway said, "would you want to kill him?"

"Not really kill him," Merle continued. "But he was sort of crazy. He had all kinds of rules. We had to stand a certain distance from him, for balance, he said. He arranged all the songs."

"Not at first," his brother interrupted. "When we first got together, he went along with us. We just play standards, you know, whether they're old or new. Whatever people are asking for. Luke, now, he was just an okay instrumentalist, but he composed. His stuff was new. He worked at music. It wasn't a hobby."

"To me neither," Merle asserted. "I work at it. And you work at it, too."

"Okay guys," Andy said. "Let's stay on track here. Who might really want Luke dead?   Any ideas about that?"

The brothers looked at each other. "One of the girls, maybe," Hank said. "They liked him but he didn't treat them so good."

"And Johnny," Merle said. "I hate to say so, but when I heard you had him in jail, I thought yeah, that could be right. Johnny could've done it."

"Why makes you think so?"

"Luke once called him Bottom-Feeder. I saw Johnny's face. I know how I would have felt."

Hank twisted in the leather chair. "Luke got us paying gigs. We wouldn't have stayed with him otherwise."

"Every now and then he'd make a real nasty jab at someone."

"At you, too?" Galway asked.

"He called me a Muckin' Musician."

"What'd you do?"

"I called him 'angel ass' and knocked him down on it."

Hank, listening to the story, had begun chewing his thumbnail. "I don't think Johnny was that mad. And I don't think he did it."

"Do you have a contender?"

"Not from our crowd."

"One of the girls might," from Merle.

"Girls don't kill like that," Hank said.

"Yeah, they do. Stabbing is a girl's method."

"How do you know that?"

"Fellows," Andy interjected again, "let's get back to Saturday night. How did Luke get home?"

The brothers looked at each other, back to Andy.

"I guess he drove," Hank said.

"You didn't give him a ride?"

"He already answered that," Merle said very softly.

Andy smiled. "Right." He made a check mark on the legal pad. "Now. Where were you last Saturday, when Luke was killed?"

"Like we told the cops, we were at the Sigma Chi house from 12:30 or so to maybe 4:00 a.m. They had their back patio and yard set up for a house concert. They had sold tickets, mostly to fraternity guys, and we played and the guest girls sang. One at a time."

"Whether they could sing or not."

"I take it," Galway said, "you didn't tell Luke about that gig."

"Nope. We just told him we were going to party."

"He didn't really like women," Hank said.

"He liked them a little," from Merle.

"He liked to *belittle* them."

"That was good."

"Fellows," Andy said.

When they were gone, Galway watched out the window until they emerged on the street outside. They were still arguing.

"Nice guys," Andy said, standing beside him. "But difficult to question."

"I'd like to meet their family someday. There are more of them, they said. Four brothers and two sisters."

"The holidays must be crazy."

"Or real nice."

"That's right," Andy said. "You were an only child."

"Back to business. I have things to do."

* * *

Galway rang Mr. Welker's doorbell, an old brass one that had sunk into the wood. It still functioned well. The door opened, and Mr. Welker was, even in that shady place, rather red faced. "Well, hello to you. Going to change the schedule I presume."

"Would you mind if I started on that post now? It's late in the day, but I painted the new one last night, at home, and it's ready to put in place. If I set it now, I could come by tomorrow afternoon, put on a second coat of paint, and we're done."

"Do it, then. You're right on top of things, aren't you? I'll help." He turned slightly toward the inside. "Edith," he called, "the repairman's here and we're going to start that job." He scurried outside, pulled the door shut. "You thought any more about digging out that tree?"

"I don't know if I could handle the thorns with just gloves. I'll look it over when we finish here."

"This won't take us long," Mr. Welker said.

It took longer than it would if Galway had been alone. Mr. Welker had a gift for spotting a weak shade of white paint, where one more stroke might even out the color. He also wanted to use Galway's level on the post.

"I've always liked levels," the old gent said. "The instrument does the work intended, and can't be misread. The chore can be complicated, but the tool, simple. A tool for everyman."

* * *

The fence again whole and its owner finally withdrawn into his home life, Galway stowed his few tools in the back of the truck. He scanned the yards as he put thin plastic gloves in one hip pocket and a pen flashlight in the other. Then he walked assuredly to the back side of Luke Michaels' house, as if assigned a task. Where the latticing overlapped, he knelt, and in seconds had slipped between two panels and was underneath the house. He let his eyes adjust to the dimness. Though the crawl space wasn't completely sealed by any means, the air here was different, cooler, moist. The musty smell of old soil was actually pleasant, a reminder of childhood, another time, another life. If it were true that a person at death could step into a dream of his own life and do it again, would he? He let that memory go, crawled forward, and almost welcomed the here and now of scrapes to his hands, elbows, and knees.

At the spot he believed to be beneath Luke's bedroom lay a

crumpled shape, like a blanket or towel. Galway carefully avoided touching it. He put on the gloves. He had bought the wrong kind, but was determined to use them up. The vinyl was thin yet hard, intended to cling tightly once on. Getting them on was the task. He rolled onto his back and swept the flashlight beam over the boards above him. He saw a line of paler, splintered wood and examined it in the beam and by touch. It was a rectangular panel. Galway pushed up against it. Again, with more force. It lifted a couple inches, but he could feel the resistance above it, an uneven pressure that might topple. He tried sliding it forward and back, but no go. Something rested on it, probably the dresser on the north side of Luke's bedroom. In alternating, tediously careful lifts, he pushed it up and forward, clearing whatever frame confined it. Right hand, left, both, he maneuvered the panel and dresser forward until the opening was almost totally cleared. He could see the back of the dresser.

With some awkward maneuvering of his long body, he finally squirmed up, into the room.

A modicum of breaking, but mostly just entering, a distinction young Johnny had made.

He suspected the panel had been nailed shut until recently. Someone had freed the panel to be lifted up.

No silence was louder than that in a place you shouldn't be. He was afraid to move and heard his own breath.

He went to the bookcase and took one of the possible journals. He leafed through the pages quickly, his intrigue gradually displaced by disappointment. It wasn't the kind of journal he had hoped. He laid it aside, took down another. Now he turned the pages more slowly. The same kind of entries. No ruminations, no comments about a day's events, no names. Galway took down another book, then another. They were the same. A writer's notebooks. Lines, stanzas. Poems. Or lyrics. He counted the volumes. Twenty-nine. He returned to the first book he had taken down. It had the most recent dates, and the last entry was one line, written two weeks before Luke had been killed. "*Tree silhouettes lace my sky. What appears in yours?*"

He became suddenly aware of the room around him, the silence of the house. He was only feet from the footboard of Luke's bed.

Suddenly he felt a familiar deep despair, waited for it to pass. When it did, as he had learned it would, he opened the book. Luke had bought expensive journals, real leather, though the style differed. His handwriting—printing, actually, small caps all the same height—was fine, almost mechanically precise. These entries had mattered to him. How long had Luke done this? He checked the date in the first volume. Twelve years ago. Luke would have been thirteen or so. Galway studied the writing on the first page. It was good then, too. Did handwriting change from puberty to adulthood? He really didn't know. He had never thought about it.

Galway reconnoitered the house slowly. The windows weren't simply locked. Each was also held fast by a nail through the sash. Each one except the window in the laundry room, through which Johnny—and possibly someone else—had entered. Beneath that window was a narrow, dark streak. He looked closely at the window sash. A hole had been drilled through this sash, too, but there was no nail. He spotted it in seconds, on the shelf above the washer. Someone had removed it, had deliberately left the window open. It could have been Luke, but Galway thought not.

He returned to the bedroom, stuck the two most recently dated journals inside his back waistband and tucked his shirt tightly around them. He exited the way he had come, from below, lifting the dresser back over the opening and letting the skirt of the piece bring the panel almost into position, then, tediously, with fingertips, finessing it the rest of the way. He couldn't be certain that the dresser was exactly where it had been but it couldn't be far off.

Almost prone on his belly, using elbows for traction, he headed for the lattice opening. Doubtless at least one snake lived under here. They could cling to a flat surface, thus could even be above him. Undisturbed soil was filled with old spores, too. What had his movements loosened? He kept his lips clenched.

Why would a murderer go to such trouble? Why not break a window or jimmy a door? Maybe the murderer hadn't come this way. Only Galway. Idiot.

He was relieved to be in the open again, but found he was a mass of itches and stings. His palms and knees hurt. At home, he called Andy and explained that he had checked under Luke Michaels' house. "There's a possible entrance to the bedroom from the crawl space, and there's a towel or rug down there. Maybe it's been there for years, but maybe not. Maybe it'll have blood on it. Let's hope it's not Johnny's."

"You didn't happen to go inside the house, did you? From this crawl space entry?"

"That would be stupid."

"So you did. Okay."

"Listen, Andy, I need access to all the journals in Luke's bookcase. Is that possible? Would you try to get possession or just the right to examine them? I need to look at every page. Maybe you could help."

"Why didn't you look at them while you were in there?"

"Stop joking around."

"You don't mean that. Joking is our best definition of the conversation at the moment."

* * *

Johnny thought the visitor would be his dad but the disappointment lasted only a second. He was so glad to see the musician and didn't feel so much a flunky and a hanger-on. He was told his father was waiting on the other side of the glassed room and would be coming in next. "He told me to go ahead, since I was here first." So Johnny had a welcome visitor and a soon-to-welcome visitor. It was almost like he had become popular and was being treated with respect. He couldn't bear thinking it was pity or anything close to that. Couldn't bear it. There was an edge to the pleasure, too, a serious one since he couldn't walk out with them. Couldn't take their hand or get in a pocket or sneak out in a shadow. He didn't want a series of farewells.

"I want to ask a favor of you, though you're not in too good a spot to do it."

"Whatever I can do," Johnny said. "I'm happy to. I mean it." And he did. Saying it was almost like freedom.

* * *

Mrs. Dunbar handed the Fallen Angels video to Galway, then gestured at the journals he had placed on her kitchen table. "I'm a little done in right now, or I would look through those with you. I do *want* to read them. I could probably stay up all night. But I've got to call a halt to myself. I'm getting too caught up in ugliness, and it can take you over. Don't laugh, Galway. Everything you do goes into what you are, and you can change the balance. Ugliness begets ugliness."

"I'm not really laughing, Mrs. Dunbar, not in a bad way. I agree with you."

"A person can even get addicted to being excited. I want calmness to be a part of my nature."

"It is. You calm me down. Often."

"Good. Right now, I'm going to calm *me* down." She looked again at the journals. "Reading them probably won't hurt you. So tell me what you find." She started to add, "If it's important," but realized that she would want to know whatever he found. She couldn't bear to be left out now. She was too excited. Like Zeena. Well, not yet. Not exactly. Poor Zeena. It would be terrible to feel under attack constantly, from the entire universe.

When Galway left, she brought from her night stand her Bible, black-leather bound, hefty, inherited from her mother. The birth records ended, unfortunately, with her. She placed it on the coffee table, which, admittedly, was like leaving a weapon handy before inviting a threatening guest. Then she went to her car, parked beneath a small carport at the side of the house, and brought in the library books. She placed them in the floor. She knew the position of the books didn't matter. They were just paper and glue and couldn't hurt anyone. She turned on a few lamps throughout the house, then brought a tea towel into the living room. She placed it across her lap and took up the first book. She wasn't a witch. She wasn't even actually dabbling. She was researching—rather, she would be in a few moments. She would begin with herbs, a lighter subject she already knew something about.

* * *

Galway read in his living room, his feet propped on a hassock. At first, he occasionally wrote a line or more on a legal pad, but gradually he just read, turning pages and back-turning, back-turning more. He found a few kid's poems, one about a tree toad. Nice. He read on. It was odd that a man who was careless with vehicles and whose home was only moderately well kept, would have maintained such a meticulous journal. He found no corrections, no strike-overs. He held a few pages under the lamp, looking for any shading of erasure. Maybe the ink was so erasable it left no trace. He tried erasing one letter. The ink was definitely permanent.

He sat down again. Many, many backside pages were blank, some were filled thoroughly. He counted the pages with any writing at all. Combining the two journals, considering front and back as two pages, 177 pages had entries. Galway did a quick calculation. If Luke had, say, thirty journals, each with 100 entries, he had 3000 pieces. If he had begun the journals about ten years ago, that meant an average of 300 pieces a year—a little short of one a day. That was easily possible, particularly if a kid fancied himself a writer. Many famous people had scheduled a daily production. Why not a poem a day? A song? So, it was feasible and even understandable.

Galway thought of his own interest—his collections, the tunes he hummed, recognized. If he wrote down every song—or parts of songs—he knew, could he fill volumes? Yes. Maybe every music lover in the world could fill volumes. And composers were music lovers beyond just desire. They *did* instead of dreamed.

He stacked the journals on the hassock, sat looking at them. It would feel good to have a physical presence of your ephemeral art, floating thoughts, something you could lift and appreciate the weight of, the sight of.

He opened the first one again, looked for a particularly sentimental piece he had noted earlier, untitled, on the backside of a page.

> *We sashay across the floor*
> *A summer breeze comes through the door.*
> *The moon's high outside*

But we can't stop to walk
We're lost in these steps.
The shy I love you so waltz.
The shy I love you so waltz.
We dance instead of talk.
I don't dare to speak
This love's made me weak.
The shy I love you so waltz.
How light is the touch of your hand.
It's stealing my whole self away.
We've whole lives to share
But we can't pause to talk
We're living this song
The shy I love you so waltz.

Galway thumb-fanned a few pages, read a line. "*The water shattered into sunlight.*" He thumbed forward again. "*You tear a thousand petals.*" Those two pieces seemed akin to one another. Maybe it was tone. He compared other passages.

"*Cut the dreaming, cut some slack.*"

"*My life's a derringdo, doll, until I daring die.*"

Same author? Maybe. He didn't know. Twenty-nine books of parchment paper, meticulously inscribed. Luke valued the very word itself. Maybe he collected words and lines the way other people collected artifacts and reprints of visual art. But reprints carried the original artist's name. Galway closed the journal, picked up the remote and turned on the Fallen Angels video.

Listening was not possible. His body was through with music or attending to anything. Galway went upstairs, showered again, convinced that something had bitten him repeatedly. His back burned. He rubbed calamine lotion over his entire body, except between his shoulder blades which, of course, was where it was most sorely needed.

He went to bed. Tomorrow was Saturday. He would finish Mr. Welker's post, consider the thorny thorn tree, and spend the rest of the day at home, designing a tasteful table-chair for a small dog, so it could lie next to its owner's chair, at hand level, and be petted without effort on the part of dog or mistress. He fell asleep with lines flitting in and out of his mind like disjointed conversation. *"All the fireflies on a hot summer night, they just blink their short life flames." "The moon is so slow. How still is this night." "Carved two rosewood rocking chairs, caught rainwater for my hair." "Milo's got the blues. His very soul feels bruised." "Makes love like he's got wings." "The shy I love you so waltz."*

* * *

The next afternoon, while sanding the rounded edge of a small table top, he paused and focused on the Fallen Angels tape. Luke Michaels, backed up by Merle and Hank, was singing *"if you can't be faithful, you can't be mine, the sun will still rise, darling, the moon will still shine."* Galway stopped the tape, ran it back, listened again.

Then he ran upstairs. He had heard some of that song before, on a Daring Do CD. He found the CD with "Hello Stranger," slipped it in the machine and punched play. In seconds, he heard the melody again, only with different lyrics, sung by Earl Wellington: *"If we can't be lovers, can we be friends, so we can see each other now and again."* The chorus for the Wellington tune, though, was *"Hello stranger, how do you do. I used to spend some good time with you."*

This was what he had noticed. But what exactly was it? A melody and rhythm of one song appearing in another, but not all the way through, and with different words.

He carried the portable player downstairs in case another passage on the Michaels' video seemed familiar. But he gave up, turned off all sound, and sanded wood. The lights in his basement workshop were uncovered and glowed too bright. Sawdust floated up, swirled, got in his hair, on his hands. He tried to remember how large that Pomeranian had been. How many steps up did it need, how long was its stride? How large was it when curled to rest?

When he began sneezing from sanding, he quit for the afternoon, listened to the Michaels' video, and found one more familiar passage. He tracked it down by switching from one track to another and another. It was Michaels copying Michaels. *"Angels all around lest we die alone,"* was part of the staccato chorus of "Turn Around Time" but was a complete song on the video. Certainly a man could copy himself.

Galway took three aspirin. He called Andy. "Any luck on getting the journals?"

"You know it's Saturday."

"I called you at home, didn't I?"

"I may get them this weekend. I may have to wait until Monday. Sheriff Bonnie says he'll get them to us as quickly as he can."

7

Stage of Darlings

ONE HALF OF BOONDOCKS WAS A RESTAURANT-BAR. DARK paneling covered the bottom part of three walls, pictures the upper part. Galway strolled along, acquiring an overview of the place's history and performers. It supported, and perhaps capitalized on, local musicians and alternative music. He recognized a few major groups that had apparently played here. In the last few feet of photos, he recognized the people he had recently learned about. The Keynotes were a casual, but sophisticated crew. Two of the members wore their hair long, but they also wore white suits. Their shirts were unbuttoned, but the image was still tasteful, perhaps swing and suavity. He recognized a tall young man from the church videos. In this photo, his left hand rested over the scroll of an upright bass as if it were an old friend. Galway imagined it was. Beside the bassist was a stocky blonde fellow with a thick moustache and a healthy smile. He held a sax with confidence. And the third man Galway had seen recently, the frazzled guitar instructor at the Musicians' Arte. He still looked frazzled, sitting between a double-decker keyboard and a set of drums. He was obviously one of those most enviable people, multitalented. The Daring Do photo was a pleasure to examine. All three girls were striking, but the petite, dark-haired one was riveting. Even in the black and white photo, she projected energy and intensity. He bet the camera sought her out at every opportunity. That's what would happen if the camera were in his hands.

Galway stopped at the bar, ordered a white ale from the bartender, and walked to the archway leading to the dance floor. No one was dancing, but the tables around the red-tiled circle were filled, many of the guests listening closely to the young man now singing. Earl Wellington. Galway sat at a table on the first tier up. Galway understood perfectly, now, why Earl Wellington believed a voice should be unique. His own was, rich and restrained for this ballad. With a voice like that, why didn't Earl think more highly of himself? Slightly behind him, smaller but vibrant, was the girl in the photo. His sister, Galway assumed. The deep drone of her fiddle underlay Earl's vocal, like a voiced harmony. The beauty of it chilled him. Three other musicians played soft background. Galway recognized two of them. The young woman on keyboard had been on the choir video. Anne something or other. Mrs. Dunbar had named her. Anne Mercer. Right. And there was the tall young man again, playing bass for this group, too. The guitarist was the Keynote sax player, bald on top, but tied-back hair reaching his waist. He looked a pleasant sort, a little overfed, as confident with his guitar as with his sax.

The song was ending, slow enough now that Galway could hear the refrain.

> *This last heartache is a long time leaving,*
> *I may be a lifetime grieving*
> *For you, for me,*
> *for what we might be.*

Earl repeated it three times, managing to change the inflection each time. It became sadder.

"We're going to take a short break," Earl Wellington announced into the microphone. "You've been a great audience. Please hang around. We have more originals on deck, some by Beth, this fine fiddler, and some by Anne Mercer, the young lady on the keyboard."

Galway approached the band's table. His respect for them was genuine, and he wanted to compliment them as well as to learn something about Luke Michaels' and Johnny Rowland's milieu.

"Hey! How you doing?" Earl stood, shook Galway's hand. "I forgot your name."

"Galway Evans."

"Sit down. How'd you know we were playing?"

Galway sat next to the young pianist, Anne. The bass player, with a curt nod that could have been courtesy or dismissal, rose, headed toward the bar.

"I didn't," Galway said. "I just thought I'd check out this place. You have a decent sized crowd."

"The bar's pretty packed most of the time. They give bands a break."

"But the Keynotes are the regulars?"

"Yep."

"They're not here tonight?"

"Leroy is." He nodded toward the bar and the man who had left the table. "And Kenny here." He glanced at the guitarist. "They were just letting me and Beth do some of our stuff. Anne, too."

"Was that last piece one of yours?"

"Actually it was. We'll be doing some of Beth's next set. You'll hang around?"

"I sure will. It'll be a pleasure."

"My stuff's not as good as Earl's," the sister said.

She had nice olive skin, with a tinge of red along the cheeks. He didn't think it was makeup. Beneath a red headband, her eyes were absolutely solid black, her eyebrows naturally arched. She was dressed like her brother, only her black shirt was unbuttoned from the bottom to just below her breasts, the shirttails tied in back. Her jeans rested low on her hips, revealing a beautiful, supple midriff. Galway thought his hands might span the circumference of her waist.

"I doubt that," he said. "It's already better."

She smiled and he went back to his table, pleased with himself.

Galway expected the sister to be good. He had heard the Daring Do CDs. And he recognized the song. "The Desert Night Sky Waltz," a mixture of major and minor keys. But it was different in performance, here, without the other girls. The lighting turned hazy, dusty, suggesting nighttime, and she was remarkably small with Anne and Earl in the shadows behind her. Her clear voice sustained notes of the sad, mournful verse. She could truly have been by a campfire, alone, watching the moon rise unbearably slow, large, white, above a night so still it could be her eternity. Then she raised her head and the music shifted into a quick, spinning chorus. She came alive.

It was a better song as just done, Galway thought, without the others. She *was* the song. Like the rest of the audience, he didn't applaud immediately. The short silence was the best tribute.

When the applause came and ended, she smiled, bowed so deeply the fiddle bow almost touched the stage. Then she nodded at Earl and Kenny and whirled, raising the bow to the fiddle. This was a different performer altogether. The notes flew. When she lowered the fiddle to lean close to Earl for harmony, she tapped the bow against the strings. *"Do"* their voices harmonized this driving note, *"do, do, do. Go up on the mountain, call out my name. Do, do, do. Give the Devil his do, honey. Die for shame. Die for shame."* She reeled off words, notes, spun herself around, winked, locked again into harmony with her brother.

Galway waited till the song ended to wave down a waitress and order another beer.

He was glad to learn Earl's sister didn't have to be center stage. When Anne had the lead, Beth Wellington stayed at the edge of the light, kept her head down or to the side. She muted the fiddle, sometimes held it behind her, becoming an audience for the singer. Earl was a pleasing performer, too. He had a nice rapport with the audience and with the other musicians. He seemed fond of everyone, delighted with the stage, the crowd, the music, and especially with his sister. They did a traditional piece Galway recognized, "Rock, Salt, and Nails." Earl sang, Beth harmonized on the last line, and Galway felt chills. These kids were good.

Galway hung around till the end, till the instruments were being put away, the last customers out the door.

"I liked everything I heard," he said. "Absolutely."

"Tell that to the manager," Earl said. "Tell your friends, too."

"I will." Galway looked at the bass player, spoke although the man wasn't looking back. "And you, Leroy, you have a fine voice. I'd like to hear more."

"Thanks." Now he looked up.

"You have anything out? A CD?"

"Not this kind of stuff."

Anne Mercer spoke. "He's got a religious CD."

"Spiritual," Leroy said.

"Spiritual," Anne shrugged. "Whatever." She spoke to Galway. "It's very good."

"Is it in the music store?" from Galway.

"No. It's at The Loft."

"That's a Christian teahouse," Earl said. "Down the street from my place."

"I'll come by," Galway said, looking at Leroy. "Are you there every day?"

"It's just open from eleven to three."

"Tomorrow, too? Sunday?"

"One to three."

"So," Galway said, including them all with a glance, "until the next time then." He met Earl's eyes. They were direct and honest. Or appeared to be.

"You bet," the young man said, and extended a hand. "Next time."

Galway stopped at the bar on his way out, asked for the manager.

"You're looking at him," the bartender said.

"The music tonight was really good. I think the Wellingtons could draw a crowd any time."

"I agree with you. When they want to play for the door, they can. Or for tips. I just don't make enough to pay them outright. They'd have to do the promoting."

"I understand the Fallen Angels played here last Friday night."

"Uh huh. You with the police? They've already asked about that. The line-up was Daring Do, Keynotes, Fallen Angels. Place was packed. We closed the door at midnight, and the musicians were sort of in and out. I was alone from about 1:00 to 1:30. Is that what you want to know?"

"Do you know when Michaels left, and who was still here?"

"Nope. I couldn't be real specific with the police either. These guys are in and out, up and down. They're as much customer as performer. You know what I mean?"

"I do. It's like a dinner theatre, where the actors are the waiters."

"Uh huh. Ask the musicians. They'll know."

"Do you know Johnny Rowland?"

"I do. I hear they've got him in jail."

"Yes."

"Can't hold his liquor."

"Was he here last Saturday?"

"Jesus. Who knows?" He turned to take an order from Anne

Mercer. She smiled at Galway.

"You're a good audience," she said. "We should pay you to come listen."

"You're all good."

She took the glass of soda, raised it a little and turned away.

The bartender said, "I guess the kid wasn't here. When he is, he's always buying drinks, especially for the girls."

"He favor any particular girl?"

"The gal *singers*. He may not know there's any other kind."

Galway went outside, took in a deep breath of moonlight and clear air. Bars were a full drug, if he counted everything—thoughts, music, smoke, liquor. He got in his truck, ready to be home. But on impulse, he drove to the other side of the lot, parked against a hedgerow, a lush dark-leafed plant with white blossoms. Oleander, he thought. Poisonous. Maybe most plants were. He wouldn't know.

He waited for the band members to disperse. He was here, wasn't he? He should utilize the time. Maybe he would learn something.

Earl emerged, carrying two of his sister's instrument cases. At this distance, the siblings looked very much alike in shape and features. Galway wondered if they were more alike in temperament than appeared evident. When someone else exited the side door, both the Wellingtons turned briefly. "Hey Kenny," Earl called. "Good stuff."

"Thanks."

Beth Wellington turned again, walked backwards with her hands in her pockets. She watched Anne Mercer and Leroy Atkins leave the building. Then she spun around and got in the car with her brother. They drove off.

Anne opened the back of a red station wagon, then got behind the steering wheel while Leroy gently put the bass in the back, covering it with a blanket. Something about their movements suggested they were a couple or at least had practiced some kind of togetherness. Since they left in the same direction Galway needed to take, he followed them. Even though the action was more accidental than chosen, he felt uneasy. He had never followed anyone before. "I do," he reminded himself aloud, "have to go this way."

When they left the main avenue, Galway did, too, though he slowed to let them get a short distance ahead. They stopped at a row of apartments and Galway drove on by, u-turned down the street and drove slowly back. He saw Leroy carrying his bass up the walk, Anne unlocking a door. Was this their home? Or the home of one? It was a low, bare-front building, a light by each door, a long narrow concrete walkway like a suggestion of a porch. He drove by again. Outside the door Anne and Leroy had entered was a ragged welcome mat. To the side was a flowerpot with a straggly, half-dead something. It signified at least an attempt at homemaking. He was fairly sure it was Anne's place. He parked yards down the street and rolled down his window. He must remember to keep a thermos of coffee handy if he planned to stake anybody out.

About an hour later, his eyes burning for sleep, he saw Anne Mercer leave. So the car was hers and this residence was Leroy's. Not much reward for his efforts, except a duty met.

Galway went home. He flicked on the kitchen light. He could never get this room bright enough, especially at night. He didn't like night time. He drank two glasses of ice water, filled the glass again and carried it upstairs, leaving the kitchen light on. He wanted to shower, clear his head, but he sat down on his bed, put the glass on the night stand. He could still see the musicians, hear their voices. Musicians were a tribe apart. The music, even unmade, must flow through them constantly, enriching everything they did. He'd never know. He'd never been in love, either.

He lay back, just for a moment, to rest his eyes. He fell asleep and dreamed of posts that were extremely tall and turned into ladders that made music and then disappeared into the ground, the wrong direction suddenly made right. When he woke, he was on his side in the center of the bed, facing the night stand. The glass held only water, no ice, and the room, in spite of the drapes, had a glow that indicated dawn was filtering into the house. He had slept for hours, but he felt he could sleep more. He wasn't ready to be awake. He closed his eyes against the dawn glow. He remembered his dad and mother always sleeping on their sides, nestled. Dying like that. He sat up, rubbed his head briskly. Now what did he have planned for today? What was first? Where would . . .

Someone was knocking on his back door. Rattling it and knocking. He hurried downstairs. "Coming," he called. "Coming." He thought, *Mrs. Dunbar. Crisis.* "Coming!"

8

Lies and Lyrics

IT WASN'T MRS. DUNBAR, BUT THE TALL, DARK-HAIRED GIRL, Anne, disheveled and at least a little piqued.

"You followed us last night," she said.

The blunt statement startled him. He wasn't accustomed to that except from his neighbor. "I'm not good at stealth. I hope it didn't worry you."

"No. It could have, but I know you and Mrs. Dunbar are friends. Could I talk to you?"

"Of course. I'm sorry." Galway pushed open the screen door. "Come in." He preceded her into his kitchen. "How do you know Mrs. Dunbar and I are friends?"

She rubbed her right wrist absentmindedly, as if twisting a bracelet. "Mrs. Dunbar goes to my church. Word gets around. She talked to Father Madison. You talked to Earl."

"How do you know she talked to Madison?"

"*Father* Madison. His secretary's a friend of my mother's. As for Earl, he told everyone. We knew you were an attorney before you even came to the Boondocks." She looked around the kitchen, toward the dim living room. "This is a giant house. You live here alone?"

He nodded. "How did people take it, that I'm an attorney?"

"Some of us are interested. You probably mean did anyone act guilty. No. That's because no one in our group is."

"You know them all personally?"

"Sure. Earl's been a friend for a long time. Beth, too, I guess. The girls in her band are students at the college. They're into degrees more than music."

He indicated a chair. "You said you wanted to talk. You might as well be comfortable."

After a longing glance at the door, which Galway assumed meant she wanted to leave, she sat down. He took a pitcher of orange juice from the refrigerator. "Would you like some while the coffee's brewing?"

"No."

"You know, you came here. I didn't summon you." He poured a small glass of juice for himself, sat so she was to his right, the window to his left.

"I want to talk to you about Luke," she said.

"Good. I need somebody to."

"I didn't kill him."

"All right."

"And he's a real bastard. All the way. Have you heard that?"

"Yes. In so many words."

"I thought so. I mean, I hate to say, since he's dead, but he truly was slime. A waste of space." She jerked her hand up to her lips. "Forget I said that, okay? No one is a waste of space. What I mean is, Luke didn't respect anyone at all. He'd say things sometimes, just out of the blue, that made you feel . . . worthless. He just loved music. Really loved it."

"What'd he say to you, Anne? That brought you here."

"That's not what brought me here. I wanted to tell you something else. You were following me and Leroy last night. I saw you. I'm worried about . . . something I know. Maybe you should know. Mrs. Dunbar wanted me to tell you myself."

"You told Mrs. Dunbar?"

"Just this morning. A little while ago. She sent me over here. She said it has to come from me."

"All right."

"Luke stole songs. At least he stole one. Leroy's song. Luke sold it to Modern Ministries Pathways. He got a contract and everything. He gets to cut the track, too. They may use his voice. But it's Leroy's song."

"How do you know it's Leroy's?"

"Because I saw the lyrics last year. Leroy showed them to me.

He sang the song, too, played it. I knew it was *for* me, in a way. I mean, he didn't write it for me, but he was singing it to me. It was *his*. He was . . ."

"Courting you?"

"Yeah. Luke's the son-of-a-bitch. Not Leroy." Her direct gaze dared him to contradict.

"All right. That's what I've heard so far. No dispute."

"I don't want to get Leroy in trouble."

"I can't guarantee that won't happen."

"I don't want to be setting Leroy up. I thought somebody should know about the song, and it's my fault Luke got it. That's all I really wanted to say. Luke got the song because of me. I had the words. I sang it for him, played it, did it again."

"What I don't get," Galway said, "is how the song could be for you but Luke sold it as a spiritual."

"Leroy writes songs that work two ways. They're to God. That's first. I guess. But they're to *people*, too."

"Oh. Come to think of it, that's a time-honored tradition."

"Maybe so, but in our crowd it's Leroy who writes them that way. I wouldn't tell you it was Leroy's song if it wasn't. I don't like this myself. I'm just trying to do the right thing. He's a good guy." Her cheeks were flushed. "I don't think he could do anything mean at all. But somebody should know about the song. Just in case."

Galway understood. In case Leroy was involved, she had to speak, but she believed—or fiercely wanted to—that he wasn't guilty. "Go on. Did Leroy find out? What did he do?"

"I think he hated me for a while, when he realized I'd shown the song to Luke. Luke sang it at church. First, he gave the music to Miss Miles, or I guess he did, and she liked it. She printed the music for all of us, and said it was a song by Luke Michaels, and that he would be doing the solo. Leroy said, 'that's not Luke's song. That's my song.' She asked what he meant and Leroy said he had written it and he didn't know how Luke got it. Luke said he had written it almost a year before and could prove it. I knew that wasn't true."

"Did you say so?"

"No. I should have." She fell silent, took a sip of coffee. "Leroy took off. I guess because I didn't say anything. He left the building. I should have followed him, but I didn't."

"Why didn't you back him up? Was it because you were seeing Luke then?"

She shook her head.

"But you were wanting to?"

"Yes." She was apparently ashamed of it. "We had planned a date. Anyhow. The choir practiced the song and it did sound different, enough that I sort of decided it wasn't Leroy's melody, especially since the words were changed a little, too. I was rationalizing."

"Did you ever talk to Leroy about this?"

"He came by my place about a week later, and I told him what had happened. He wanted to know if I was seeing Luke and I told him that I was, a little. Nothing serious. That's because nothing but music was ever serious to Luke. Leroy wanted me to tell Miss Miles that the song belonged to him. I said I would do that. I didn't want to, but I would. He left. Later he returned and said to forget about talking to Miss Miles. He didn't think it was important enough to make it church gossip, which might happen. He said I didn't have to sacrifice myself for him. He meant that. He hung around till I agreed to let it go, and he left. That's when I began taking him more seriously. I mean, I was still crazy about Luke, but Leroy was the nice guy. I knew that."

"Did it come up again?"

"No. We—the choir—practiced the song like we did the others, and we taped it at the church like we did the others. Leroy even sang. If he ever said anything to Luke, I don't know."

"You didn't want to know," from Galway.

"Yeah."

"Do you remember any of the lyrics? Could you write them down for me?"

"Well. Let me think . . . Sure, some of them, anyhow. Why?"

"I prefer knowing something specifically instead of in general. And I may have heard that song on a tape. I want to check."

She nodded. "Okay."

He brought a legal pad from his study, read over her shoulder as she wrote.

"I'm leaving a few spaces," she said, "when I can't remember."

"That's all right. Just do the best you can."

When she finished, she pushed the pad away.

"Were you," Galway said, "still seeing Luke recently? Till his death?"

"No. I quit seeing him about six months ago. He was acting a little . . . not interested. Bored. He stopped calling. He didn't return my calls—I only called him a few times. I've got some pride. At the Boondocks one night, I saw I had been replaced."

"He brought somebody else?"

"No. He was just *with* somebody else. Beth."

"Oh. I see."

"Yeah. That happens in bands. You know. You harmonize, and you think it's love."

"Anything else?"

Anne seemed uncertain, then said, "No. I said what I came to say."

"You realize I'll need to talk with Leroy?"

"Yeah. I may lose him after all." She focused on Galway. "You're really tall. Tall as Leroy."

"At least that. My mother wished it on me."

He walked outside with her, strolled across thick grass, heard the steady, easy roar of a lawnmower down the street. The early sun bounced glints from her car.

"You take good care of your car. I thought it was probably Leroy's."

"He doesn't drive," she said, opening the door. "Well, he drives, but he doesn't have a car right now. He thinks walking is healthier for the body and the country. Walking and cycling."

"You take him everywhere?"

"Only if he has to take the bass or other equipment. He walks, runs. That's how he stays so skinny." Her gaze quickly swept Galway and she corrected herself. "So thin, I mean. And his brother drives a taxi."

Galway leaned down to the door window. "We're trying to find Luke's car or cars. You know anything about them?"

"The old Ford wasn't at his place? He had it at Boondocks on Saturday." She cocked her head. "I think I remember it there. You might ask Johnny. He likes cars. He might even know the license plate number."

When Galway went inside, he read Leroy's lyrics. Anne had apparently remembered most, if not all, of the song.

How sweet grows the air
where you walk, and when you speak
words rise like music, to start my breath, my heart
        my hope.
I can love.
You gave me this, you light the dark,
send fleeing all that weighs a spirit down.
Let me love in your shadow.
Your light is too bright for me now.

Yes, Galway had heard this before. It had been one of Luke's solos with the choir—but it had belonged to Leroy.

He ate an apple and a few saltines, tried to recall Anne's song from last night, a snappy little swing piece. *"I got leaving in the soles of my feet, not staying in the key to the door . . . ."*

Sharp little gal.

He needed to talk to Leroy. Meanwhile, he could go back to sleep. Or he could type the CD lyrics into the computer for reference. A guide to stolen lyrics.

He enjoyed it. He couldn't transcribe the melodies, but he was familiar with them all. When he looked at particular lyrics, the melody rose in him. He wondered how it would feel to have *written* them and have the words and melody be part of who you were. Then he wondered how Luke felt, knowing they weren't part of him at all. But maybe they were. Maybe that's what Luke was trying to do. Acquire a beauty missing in him by stealing it.

* * *

Sunday morning, Mrs. Dunbar attended church precisely to listen closely to the choir. Their taped performances had made her realize how little reward they had. These people actually practiced, and came early to don the heavy robes and to queue up, to march in singing. For some special services, they had to stand outside, waiting for a procession to begin. At the very least, they deserved an audience of parishioners. Mrs. Dunbar chose the second pew, closer than she had ever sat, but at its far end, where the ceiling fan's draft couldn't reach her. Sitting still beneath a constant breeze was a mild torture.

When the procession entered, Mrs. Dunbar stood, head bowed, and kept her eyes on the hymnal in her hands. She wouldn't let her mind wander inappropriately here. When she looked up, though, and saw Betty Miles, she remembered the church albums at the rectory. She gasped slightly. Why hadn't she noticed sooner? Mrs. Dunbar felt someone staring at her. She drew her attention from Betty, looked at the choir. Myra Wren's tiny face beamed from the center of the front row. Mrs. Dunbar waved discreetly. Myra was a dear heart. She was glad for Myra, for many people, that voices didn't age quickly.

Mrs. Dunbar kept her mind on the service except for brief moments. When Rosie's little boy darted from the children's service, under the front pew, and tried to squirm past Mrs. Dunbar, she grabbed his belt in the back, and held him for his mother. When Rosie had shuttled him to children's class, she returned to sit by Mrs. Dunbar.

"I need a leash," she whispered.

Mrs. Dunbar caught herself just short of saying, "They make them for children," which might have been taken painfully to heart by Rosie and forever regretted by Mrs. Dunbar.

Another brief lapse occurred when Lester Foley cranked open one of the side windows, leaving a section of the parking lot in view. Mrs. Dunbar's attention drifted toward the opening. She looked from it to Betty Miles and again felt uneasy, nagged by another memory.

She heard Father Madison say, "Let us pray." She knelt on the prayer bench. "Dear Father," he said, his tone so humble and loving that she felt her thoughts giving in to his. This is what church was about. She listened.

After church, outside the entrance, she waited on Rosie and her son. She walked with them to Rosie's car. "Do you know if Luke Michaels and Betty knew each other before she came here?"

"No. They never said anything about it. Why?"

"I just wondered how Luke came to our choir." Even if they were related, who was she to start talk?

"Ask her."

"I may. But not today."

"She may be more than our choir director very soon."

"I thought so," Mrs. Dunbar said.

"I'm sorry about your nephew," Rosie said. "When I heard that he was your kin, I felt really bad for you. You like young people so much. It must have been a deep hurt."

Mrs. Dunbar nodded, unable for a few seconds to do other than smile. Finally, "Thank you. It is hard, but he won't be in jail long because he didn't do it."

Now it was Rosie's turn to nod, as if innocence were a given, at least in this conversation.

"My sister works at the jail and she said he must be a nice kid because the deputies speak well of him and he's had some nice visitors."

"What visitors? Do you know?"

"I know a gentleman left cigarettes and money for him, and his aunt left a package for him yesterday."

"I'm his only aunt."

"Oh. I don't know then, who she was."

Rosie's son dropped down, which freed him from his mother's touch, and ran back toward the church. Rosie took off after him.

Mrs. Dunbar would have loved such a problem.

She hadn't been to the jail. What aunt? What was in the package? Her mind scouring for possibilities, she absentmindedly returned to the building, waiting on Myra. She wanted to compliment her for the choir and to pry gently about Galway's work on Myra's roof. He was such a willing and ardent worker, she felt, and wanted to insure that Myra felt the same, even if it took a bit of coaching.

With her thoughts briefly side-tracked, a solution to the aunt question presented itself. Zeena. Who else would take a care package under a pseudo relationship? Zeena. Mother via witch. Mrs. Dunbar smiled—Zeena loved that boy, like it or not.

Myra didn't appear. Mrs. Dunbar searched her out, found her in the patio, testing the moisture of a potted plant.

"The songs were lovely," Mrs. Dunbar said. "And you looked so beautiful up there."

"You should join us, Lettie," Myra said. "You like music."

"I can't sing."

"You can so. I see you singing along with the congregation."

"Usually I'm only moving my lips. We all have our gifts, and singing is not one of mine. Besides, I wouldn't be able to stand erect, or even hold the choir book steady."

"Oh. Sorry, Letitia."

"It's perfectly all right. If I wanted to be a choir girl, I'd have a chair put beside the first tier." It wasn't true, but the attitude it conveyed was accurate. She didn't want Myra feeling insensitive.

Myra talked about a particular strain of hibiscus. Mrs. Dunbar did listen, but she also thought how graceful Myra's slender hands were, how fine her silvery hair. And she thought, too, how Betty Miles had stood here earlier in the week, not going inside though obviously that's where she was headed. People with secrets often forgot what acting natural was, because nothing was natural anymore.

"See this?" Myra said, holding up a finger smudged with black potting soil. "It's so dry it brushes clean." She demonstrated her statement. "And only then can I add a smidgeon of water. Most people would over-water it."

"I do better with sturdy plants that can survive my caretaking."

Myra's slight laugh was warm, friendly. They had liked each other for a long time, but never socialized. Theirs was an infrequent, but always pleasant and familiar encounter.

* * *

Leading up to the Loft was a narrow stairway with shallow steps ending, without door or landing, at the next level. At the top step, Galway was in the center of the restaurant, the counter along a wall some yards behind him, and a scattering of round tables before him. A few young people were having lunch. It was, surprisingly, a pleasant place. High windows, three of them stained glass, wrapped around the room and light flooded through, adding prisms of color here and there. It was a little mystical.

Leroy was behind the counter, putting clean glasses in rows before a mirror. His reflection acknowledged Galway's approach, but he continued his work till all the glasses were aligned. Then he turned around.

"I guess I know why you're here," he said, mildly.

"I said I'd be by for one of your CDs."

"Right. That's not what I meant, though." He nodded toward a display case at the end of the counter. "I only have one. It's down there. You want to hear it?"

"I want to *buy* it. I can listen to it later."

"Okay." He went for the CD, placed it before Galway. "Anything else?"

"I'd like to talk with you a few minutes?"

"That's what I expected."

"I could have lunch, too. You have chili?"

"Not in the summer."

"Pity. What's the fastest?"

"Tuna."

"That'll do." Tuna was recently his lot in life.

Galway paid for the CD and meal, then took a table near the counter. He leafed through a Bible. One was on every table. According to the front page, this particular Bible was given to a girl named Shirley Chaffen by Carmellia Chaffen. He wondered how it came here. Another mystery for another day.

Leroy set a tray on the table, pulled out a chair. "I brought you coffee and water, save having to ask."

"Both are fine." Galway pulled the tray closer. "This looks good."

"What do you want to ask me, Mr. Evans?"

There was no animosity at all in the voice. Leroy had a direct gaze, brown, soft eyes, a rather rugged, square face, high cheekbones, smooth olive skin, and black, thick, straight hair, pulled back with a band at the neck. Whatever his heritage, strength in body and mind had come forward. Galway felt an instinctive like and trust. But somebody had to be guilty. Maybe it was going to be Johnny, after all. "I hear Luke stole one of your songs, and maybe more. A girlfriend?"

"He claimed one of my songs, that's true, but it's not that big a deal. It happens all the time in the music world. Old melodies get claimed under new titles. 'El Condor Pasa' was supposedly a Peruvian folk song. Accidental stealing is an occupational hazard. After a person hears enough songs, words come together and he's not sure where he got them. I'm not even sure of myself."

"Does that mean you weren't angry with Luke?"

"No. I was angry," said matter-of-factly. "And I still am. But I'll get over it. Anger undoes a person if he holds onto it."

"Anne told me Luke had sold *your* song, had a contract, and was cutting a track for the CD. He was setting up a future using your work without permission. That's not easy to ignore."

"People use other people all the time. It's a characteristic of the human species."

"Including you?"

"Including everybody. We can try not to. Sometimes we fail."

"Do you think Luke stole work from other people?"

"Probably."

"Who?"

"Everyone he ever knew."

"You know what I mean, Leroy. Somebody killed him. And it's your work he was going to make money from right now. As far as we all know, that is."

A muscle along Leroy's left jaw twitched, but he didn't say anything.

"You're the one with the most right to be angry. Maybe you confronted him. Maybe you went there to talk and things got out of hand."

"I didn't confront him. I should have. Maybe none of this would have happened."

"Would you explain that? What could you have stopped?"

"I don't know."

"Who had a better reason than you?"

"I'll tell you one thing," Leroy said. "Johnny Rowland didn't do it."

"How do you know?"

"Johnny couldn't do it. He's more kid than his age would make him. He just wants to hang around, maybe pick up some talent or at least have talented people like him. He doesn't have high aspirations, though he's smart enough."

"He broke into Luke's house. Maybe he got pushed into doing something he normally wouldn't."

"He didn't like Luke. He might steal from Luke to get him. You know—to pay the guy back for something."

"And you would understand that."

He leaned forward, forearms on the table. He shook his head. "Yes. I would understand that."

"Did you set him up?"

He didn't answer.

"You don't believe in lying, do you, Leroy? You work here, in a Christian café. You record this." Galway indicated the CD. "You believe in telling the truth. Why hold back?"

"I'd tell the truth if that was the right thing to do. Sometimes it isn't. Sometimes lying is a kinder act than honesty."

"We agree there—truth is relative."

"Human truth."

"Did you kill Luke Michaels?"

"No."

"Okay." Galway sighed. "I don't think you could be guilty and not confess to it, not with Johnny in jail. But I also think you know who did and you don't want to trade that person for Johnny."

"I've got work to do, Mr. Evans."

"You need to tell me what you know, Leroy. Somebody has to help Johnny."

Leroy nodded at the tray. "You want me to wrap that?"

"No." Galway opened a paper napkin, wrapped it around the sandwich. "Come on. Tell me something. Take some responsibility."

"I *am* taking responsibility. And I'm sorry about Johnny."

He walked away, began clearing tables. He dropped the gathered tips into a jar at the end of the counter. Galway finished his sandwich hurriedly, drank the water, and carried a generous tip to the jar. He read the message taped on the glass: "for Grace Christian Fellowship." He reached for his wallet. In the mirror, Leroy watched. Galway nodded, turned to look at the real Leroy, said "thanks," and headed for the stairway.

Outside, Galway muttered "It must be a woman." Leroy was a mature young man, with high morals—unless he was pretending— but he was also male, and very likely that fierce protection rose from the natural desire to safeguard the weaker, and perhaps the innocent. Who? It could be Anne Mercer. But she seemed as much in the dark as anyone and obviously believed that Leroy might have been the murderer. Maybe she was a consummate actress. Galway started up the street, his shadow small and hugging close at this noontime. He saw the signs along Fourth, the striped blue and burgundy awning above the bread-and-soup place. He turned around. He didn't need to eat and he didn't want to see Earl Wellington just now. He needed to sort out whose songs were whose.

He headed home. Should he tell Mrs. Dunbar about the conversation with Leroy? Yes. Leroy had expressed faith in Johnny. That spoke well for both young men. If Leroy had been Luke's assailant, why would he defend Johnny? It would make more sense if he had cast Johnny to the wolves.

A message from Andy awaited him. He called him back.

"I have the journals," Andy said, "all twenty-seven of them. But they can't leave my possession. You can meet me at my office, home, or I can bring them to you, but where they go so go I."

"Could you bring them here? We could work in the dining room."

"You got it. I have more news. You're going to like this, or most of it. The rug has no blood other than Luke's. The knife, though, tells a different story. The blood is from two different sources, but neither source is Johnny. They couldn't get any clear prints. The knife had been wiped. It wasn't *clean* by any means, but other than the blood, there wasn't anything usable. The rug still may provide a lead or two. They found different kinds of hair."

"Luke had a lot of guests."

"I know. But if none of the hair is Johnny's . . ."

"I guess I can pass this information on to his aunt?"

"Sure."

Galway did so, and he stayed for a while to tell her about the knife and rug. They sat on her back steps. His garage was just across the alley, down a few yards. He saw birds alight on the corner and disappear inside. Mrs. Dunbar rose to investigate something moving along the bricks next to the house.

"A frog," she said. "Pretty fat." She sat down.

"What's a tree toad?" he asked. "Is it different from a tree frog?"

"I've wondered that myself. The one my mother called a tree toad was very tiny, the size of a little finger nail. It was dry and brown, and could hide in a crack of bark. They're adorable. We have them here, but they're hard to spot. The tree toads in books, though, are green, and properly frogs. I wonder if my mother decided what it was or if different classes of people disagree about the names of things."

"Different classes of people?"

"I come from a long line of proud poverty," she said. "Some people sweep their dirt yards."

A cloud shadow floated over the back yard. He remembered another house and time, when he was lying in his room with his parents outside. He heard their voices against other pleasant sounds, cicadas, he imagined, and bird calls.

"What made you think of tree toads?" Mrs. Dunbar asked.

"I read a poem about one, by Luke."

"Oh. That's sad."

9

Shadow of Love

AT HIS DINING TABLE, GALWAY PUSHED ONE OF THE STACKS toward Mrs. Dunbar and another toward Andy. "These lyrics are by Beth Wellington, her brother Earl, and Leroy. At least, that's the credit on the CDs. This stack," he touched papers next to him, "has the songs that may actually be Luke's, or mostly Luke's. I got the words from the Fallen Angels video. There may have been other musicians involved—Beth's partners, and Luke's—but for now, we'll just worry about the ones credited on the recordings. We'll check them against Luke's journals."

"Have you considered," Mrs. Dunbar said, "that Luke may have copied as a technique of learning? That used to be the accepted method. Of course the students were copying the work of masters."

"Maybe Luke started out that way. But there's an oddity about the journals I haven't mentioned. They ostensibly date back to when he was fourteen, but the handwriting is the same in every one of them. Is that common? To write the same at twenty-four as you did at fourteen?"

"I don't know," Andy said. "I think my handwriting is the same. Illegible."

"And I don't know either," Mrs. Dunbar said. "But I assume there would be a significant change, from personality if nothing else. Maybe he began keeping journals when he was young, and then later rewrote them. I can understand someone doing that. It's a kind of neatness."

"That makes sense." Galway sat down, took a cup from the tea service in the center of the table. On either side of it were stacks of Luke's journals. "So. This is what we do. First read the lyrics I just gave you. Then take one of the journals and skim it, looking for something similar, maybe only a line, maybe an entire stanza."

"Let's try to get through them all this afternoon," Andy said. "I don't like being responsible for so many pieces. I'd swear there are more already than I brought in."

Mrs. Dunbar moved to the other side of the table, so she could see out the window. On the high fence enclosing a small courtyard, a crow strutted. In her upbringing, crows meant death.

I hope that's not a sign," she said.

Andy turned to look. "Isn't a crow a bad omen?"

"Someone's already dead," Mrs. Dunbar said. "If he's the omen, he's late. Or. . . I wish I hadn't said anything."

"Time is wasting," Galway said.

"That's a horrible saying." Mrs. Dunbar gathered the stack of Luke's own work and sat back down.

A short time later, Andy exclaimed "Hey! I've already found one. Listen to this."

He held a loose page in his right hand. "This is from the lyrics: *I return with all my heart, every gift, all my art, as song to you. Let me live, love, within your sound, let me hear, heart, your music round.*" Andy turned to the journal he held open with his left hand. "And from the journal, written one Saturday evening supposedly two years ago, at six p.m., is a poem titled 'Music Round.' The last stanza goes like this: *'I return with all my heart, every gift, all my art, as song to you. Let me live, love, within your sound, let me hear, heart, your music round.'* Not even one letter variation."

"The lyrics were by Leroy Adkins?" from Galway.

"You got it. Have you memorized them all?"

"I've listened to the tapes a lot. And I typed every word you just read."

Andy tore a strip of paper from his sheets, placed it in the journal. "Maybe Leroy stole it from Luke."

"Maybe. But I doubt it. When Luke heard a song he fancied, he entered it in his journal, dating it in the past, so it seemed to belong to him. Crazy. But in most cases, no one would have known—only if a song made it really big, and it might be his version that did make it."

"I wonder why he copied, "Andy said, "when he could write

lyrics himself?"

"We don't know yet that he *could* write," Mrs. Dunbar said. "And even if he did write some of these, maybe he didn't think they were very good. Maybe he was a singer who wanted to be a composer."

"Maybe he was just a thief," Andy said. "No extenuating circumstances, no bad childhood—just a thief."

"There's always an extenuating circumstance."

"Good for you," Mrs. Dunbar said to Galway, then spoke to Andy. "Are you representing Johnny for free?"

"Of course he's not," Galway said quickly. "There's a fund for cases like this."

"Rates are arbitrary, Mrs. Dunbar," Andy said. "For friends, the charges are minimal, sometimes just court costs."

"What about now, when you're going over these journals with us?"

"It's free."

"Is that true?" Mrs. Dunbar asked Galway.

"Of course, or Andy wouldn't say it."

"What about this fund you mentioned?"

"It's a genuine fund," Andy responded, "for clients we want to represent."

Mrs. Dunbar looked from one to the other of them. "I got it," she said. "But I'm not broke, and if Johnny's parents don't pay you, I will."

Andy lifted his eyebrows.

"Among the three of us, then," Galway said, "we have it well covered, so let's just get on with the work of it."

"Good."

They understood each other.

Mrs. Dunbar read the thirty-two songs twice. Then she took up pencil and began on the stack of lyrics that were from the Fallen Angels video. She skim read, trusting her recent memory to stop at a familiar line. When she paused, she marked the line with a pen, without examining it closer, and skimmed on.

Galway settled back with a journal. In a song dated three years before were two lines, *"you've got loving in the palms of your hands, and leaving in the back of your mind."* He couldn't be certain of the melody Luke intended, but Anne's recent tune suggested the rhythm. *"I've got leaving in the soles of my feet, not staying in the keys to the door."* Two lines, not really the same, but so close. Who was first? Was this legitimate? Could musicians do this? Maybe that's what music was, conversation in tune, borrowed lines, history, repetition.

Before he took another journal, he stood behind Mrs. Dunbar's chair and looked at her notes. She had put phrases in parentheses.

She handed him a copy of one of Luke's songs. "Many of the good lines came from somebody else's work."

"Yes, that's what I saw, too," Galway said. "And if you listen to them, which I've done, you hear bits of one melody woven into another."

"There are only so many scales," Andy said.

"But millions of human touches," Mrs. Dunbar responded.

Galway supposed that was true. The possible melodies were endless. Maybe a few of these, even more, were actually Luke's.

A few hours later, the crow still interested in the patio, they had finished a first examination of all the journals. It was, in Galway's mind, enough. According to Luke Michaels' records, he had written most of these songs, and had done so from one to six years before the date on the CD. Yet these journal entries had been made in a short period of time. It looked like he was a special kind of thief, craving and claiming an artistry he didn't have, or didn't have to his satisfaction.

"Well, he didn't get every song his colleagues wrote," Galway said. "But I think he got most of them, by buying the CDs and working backwards. The CDs are locally recorded. He wouldn't have had to fight a real recording company. I doubt there's a formal copyright on any of these."

"He probably didn't give a damn," from Andy. "The other musicians had to have noticed this. I mean, they listen to one another's recordings, right?"

"I'm sure they noticed. He may have been a little judicious about which songs he played where. Maybe it was a game, a variation on Russian Roulette."

"Find that tune and sue me."

"We're missing a journal, aren't we?" Mrs. Dunbar said. "I tried putting the journals in order, and some dates are missing, maybe eight months."

"Yep. We're missing at least one. I think it has Leroy's 'In the Shadow of Love' and maybe a few others by him."

Andy was looking back and forth at the two of them. "So Leroy Adkins was there, in Luke's house? He took a journal?"

"At least that."

"What about some of the other musicians?" Andy held up a journal. "Who else might have been there?"

"Maybe Beth Wellington," Galway said. "Two of her best pieces are missing from this collection. 'Desert Night Sky Waltz' and 'Devil Do.'"

"Maybe Luke didn't want them," Andy said.

"I doubt that," Galway said. "I imagine we haven't found them because, as Mrs. Dunbar noted, some dates are missing, and that means some journals are missing. Beth's songs are in those volumes."

Andy, beginning to stack the journals, said, "Maybe Johnny has them."

"I think not," Mrs. Dunbar said. "It would require a kind of subtlety he lacks." She didn't mean to be disparaging the young man, but she felt as if she had betrayed him and the whole family by her remark. "He's a gentle boy, though, and maybe he has abilities, depth, that I haven't acknowledged."

Andy looked relieved at this opening. "One of the first things you learn in my business is not to underestimate the abilities of anyone, especially the ability to lie. It's a survival mechanism, automatic to many, even to members of one's own family."

* * *

Johnny had received a package ostensibly from his Aunt Lettie, but he was one hundred per cent positive it was from his mother. She thought of him as a kid who liked gum, candy, cookies, and that's what was mostly here. There was a pack of cigarettes, too, that might or might not have been with the other stuff. It was all open and mixed up, though the original bag was included. The cookies were in some clinging paper, which was probably his mother's attempt to disguise her handiwork, since she used pressure-locked bags, hand-labeled with item and date. If something wasn't used in the proper time, the entire bag was inserted in another, larger bag. If that wasn't used soon, the whole thing was discarded. Freshness mattered. So did appeal. She insisted food and surroundings be rich and attractive. The old world did things right. The modern world was too bare and exposed, all skin and ugliness.

Truthfully, he did like candy, cookies, and gum, though he preferred cigarettes to all of them. Sometimes, only sweet would do, and lots of it. Sated with it. Reeking of it. He wished someone was around to see what he had been given, and with whom he could share. He had torn the bag the rest of the way open, spread it flat like a scarf on the orange table. He pulled out three cookies and laid one edge overlapping the next, as if for a guest. He hated having the emptiness of the whole pod all around him, like the bowels of a space ship abandoned somewhere with aliens outside. He went to the window, cupped his eyes so he could see the hall and part of the control desk. No one was watching him. They'd let him hang himself if he could do it with gum.

He took one of the cookies, sniffed it, dusted it, pinched a bit and put it on his tongue. That primed the pump. He ate most of them, stuck two cigarettes in his pocket and called through the intercom for a match, please. With the cigarette lighted, the deputy again out of the room, he enjoyed this gift, too. On the high, quiet television a dog found a ball in high grass and then hid with it behind a tree, only his head hidden, his wagging tail whipping a giveaway from side to side. Johnny had never been allowed to have a dog, either, because they dug up yards, messed in yards, and shed all over a house.

* * *

Sunday night, Galway stayed at home. Maybe the crow had been portending rain, because it fell, steadily, slow sheets. He worked for a while in a side room he had turned into a workshop. He rubbed a maple finish into the dog-nesting table he had fashioned. In the moist air, the piece would take quite some time to dry, but he could focus on other work with that stage done.

He was tired of music, but the house was too quiet. It was too big for him alone. Sometimes he thought he had made a mistake moving here, getting a house that would have been fine for a large family.

He looked at the next week's list of jobs. None interested him. He couldn't imagine having the energy to do any of the work. Thunder rumbled and he was glad of the sound. He enjoyed rain. His mother had also. She would open the doors if the rain wasn't slanting that direction. Right now, he would relish a storm, any kind. He showered, put on fresh clothes, and still couldn't shake the heaviness that had descended. He went to his study, where he opened the bottom drawer of his desk. He gave up. The craving was never going to end. He took out a pack, peeled back the corner fold, and tapped out a cigarette. Without hesitation, he lit it, and drew the warm, pungent, wonderfully familiar taste down into his lungs. It burned and he had the urge both to spit and to draw again. He took another draw, and another, and his body settled down. He was slightly dizzy and nauseated, which was okay. He didn't mind. Tobacco was a delight to him and always had been. He was a natural smoker. His body knew. He dropped the pack in his shirt pocket, walked to a side room, looked at the sheet rain, slow and steady, straight down.

In the dim light cast a few feet out from the house, he could see the dancing drops, splash and leap, splash and leap. He could see Mrs. Dunbar's house lights. Then he realized he could see *her*. She was in the rain, headed for the rear of his house in that twisting walk she couldn't help. No cane. He ran to the back door and down the steps.

"Johnny's in the hospital," she called weakly. "He says he's been poisoned."

Galway took her arm, which was surprisingly thin. She always wore long-sleeved shirts and slacks. She hid her fragility. "You shouldn't be out in this."

"Let's go right now." She tugged free and turned toward his garage. "Let's get to the infirmary, wherever that is."

"You won't be able to see him."

"He called me and I'm going."

Of course she was. Galway could see that. "If he was able to talk, he's not too bad off."

"He didn't talk to me. Whoever called did. A man, and it was an adult voice, said Johnny Rowland had asked him to call. Johnny was in the infirmary, ill, and believed he had been poisoned."

"Slow down. Don't let yourself fall."

"This is just mud. I'm not going to break a bone. It's not as bad as poison."

Galway ushered her under the low roof of the old stables. "I've got to get the keys. Wait here. I'll be right back."

Inside his house, he wanted to call the jail or Andy, but he suspected any delay would send Mrs. Dunbar driving off in her own car. He hurried back, relieved to find her waiting. He unlocked the BMW, opened the door for her. "We can call Andy from the jail. There won't be any traffic. It's a straight shot."

The rain glistened, caught headlights and diffused the beam. Mrs. Dunbar was silent, hands in her lap. "He'll be all right," Galway said. "Look at the big picture. This is all temporary. If he only burglarized, he may have to serve a short sentence, but maybe not even that. Maybe probation. Don't let this make you sick, Mrs. Dunbar."

"Maybe he should go into the army."

"Good. Good. That's the way to think. Enlistment is an option under some judges. We could look into that."

She didn't respond. Cars shushed by. "Has he ever mentioned enlisting?" Galway asked.

"I didn't mean it," she said. "He shouldn't have to go in the army. That's not a normal life either, not if it's an escape. Either-or is a narrow choice."

Better than none, he thought.

When he parked at the County Jail, he said, "You can wait inside, but they probably won't let you talk with him."

"I get tired of the word 'they,'" she said. "If you know who 'they' are, direct me to them."

"I'll tell them you're my assistant."

"You tell Johnny that I'm here, that I'm as close as I could get."

According to the entry guard and to the nurse on the third floor, Mrs. Dunbar could not visit Johnny. She should wait in the small lobby near the entrance. The guard led her there, though it was only feet away, then moved an orange plastic chair from inside the lobby to the outside. He sat down heavily, settling in so low that Galway expected the man knew he would fall asleep. The nurse now pointed toward the other side of the counter, and the doors beyond.

"Rowland is in that room. He's feeling pretty bad, but he wanted to see someone."

"Who telephoned his aunt?"

"Douglas." She indicated a deputy coming toward them from the opposite side of the room. She spoke toward him. "This is Rowland's attorney."

The man nodded. "He wanted his aunt. I told him they wouldn't let her in here."

"She's in the lobby."

"Good."

Galway wasn't prepared for Johnny to be actually ill. He had expected some drama, maybe nervousness. He hadn't expected an alarming paleness and sunken, burning eyes.

"Hey, fellow," Galway said, and took the offered hand. "You look pretty rugged."

"I got hold of something." He paused, breathed coarsely. "My stomach balled up like a rock. I couldn't stand up." He shook his head, turned to look toward the door.

"Your Aunt Lettie is in the lobby. No guests in here either. Same rules as downstairs. She wants you to know she came, and wants to come in."

Galway heard something behind him, and knew it was Mrs. Dunbar before he looked. "There you are," she said, forcing herself a little taller and smiling at Johnny, heading for the bed. She squeezed his hand. "It is so good to see you, Johnny." She pressed the back of her fingers to his cheek, then brushed his dark hair back from his temples. Galway realized she was checking him over. It was a mother's touch. Grandmother's. "You'll be all right," she said. Through the door panel-window the dark-haired Douglas was apparently still on guard.

Already Johnny had brightened but not enough to indicate any faking here. His eyes were still feverish.

Mrs. Dunbar rolled the adjustable table to the bed, filled a glass from the carafe. "You need ice," she said. "You're burning up."

"I ate it all." Johnny said.

"And you can eat more," she said. "It's good for you right now. Maybe this is just a virus."

"No, Aunt Lettie. Somebody tried to poison me. I know."

Galway walked around the bed. "Tell me how you know."

"I had this sack of stuff. I ate a candy bar." He took a deep breath, shuddered. "I feel pretty bad."

"I'll get ice." Mrs. Dunbar took the plastic bin, headed for the door. It opened and Douglas took the plastic container from her.

"I'll be right back," he rumbled.

"Bring ice, not water," she called after him. She returned to Johnny's bedside, flashed a concerned look toward Galway but stayed silent.

Galway was worried, too. "Who sent the candy bar?"

A shrug. "They said my dad had come and a friend had come. They gave me a sack with candy bars, sticks of gum, some cookies. A pack of cigarettes. They were all store-bought, sealed in plastic. They should have been okay. There was this dusty stuff on the chocolate. I thought it was just more chocolate, you know?"

Mrs. Dunbar slipped her hand into Johnny's. "I doubt it was poison. No one wants to hurt you, honey."

Now he was near crying. "I don't want to be in here anymore."

"Of course you don't. Who would? That may be what's making you sick."

He shook his head vehemently. "I *saw* the poison, Aunt Lettie. That dust. I think it was in the cigarettes, too. I think it was in everything. It might've killed me."

"All right," she said. "I believe you. Galway will find out who did it. Won't you, Galway?"

"If I can."

Mrs. Dunbar aligned the tissue box, then walked away. Galway, from the corner of his eye, saw her lift a shirt from a chair back, then sit down in the chair. He turned his attention to Johnny. He didn't know why anyone would want to harm Johnny. No one with any sense at all would try to send poison into a jail, in a care package. The whole incident was odd. Or was a lie. The latter seemed most likely. But Johnny was, without doubt, visibly ill.

"I don't know what's going on here, but I don't think you're faking. I'm sorry this happened."

"Me, too," with a little more force.

A rap on the door was followed by Douglas' entry, ice rattling in the container. He carried it to the bed table, spoke to Johnny. "How you doing, kid?"

"Better."

"That's good." He left without looking at Mrs. Dunbar. In his official guard's view, she couldn't exist.

"Do you know who might want to hurt you, Johnny?" Galway asked.

"Everybody likes me." Johnny attempted a smile. "Maybe Luke didn't."

"Have you remembered who might have set you up?   Who got you thinking about Luke's equipment?"

"Nobody made me do it."

"You do remember."

"I'm the one who left a trail, you know. I didn't have to do that. I was stupid. And I was stealing. No doubt about that. I didn't have any good motives going in."

"Somebody else did?"

Johnny didn't answer.

"They're leaving you to hang for a murder."

He shook his head despairingly. "I didn't murder anybody and nobody I know would set me up for one."

"I'm pretty sure it was Leroy," Galway said, and saw the flicker, immediately controlled, in Johnny's wan face.

"You're pretty sure wrong," Johnny said, but a second too late.

"One more thing. Could you have gotten in the window without using the blocks?"

"I don't know."

"Did you put the blocks there?"

The answer was too slow in coming. "Yeah. Sure. Who else?"

"Okay. Anything more?"

"No."

"Then I'll see what they're doing with your care package and get your aunt home." Galway started toward the door.

"Could you give me a couple of cigarettes?" Johnny said, a little contritely. "Just for later."

"I left a carton for you the other day."

"I only got a couple packs. They went pretty fast. The deputies let me have about as many as I want. They didn't say I had more. And what was in the sack was a different kind. Now I'm going to be afraid of anything they give me."

Galway took the newly opened pack from his pocket and handed it to Johnny. Mrs. Dunbar was watching. She stood up, folded the shirt across the back of the chair, and came forward, hand out.

"Let me have one."

"Aw, Aunt Lettie."

"I'm not going to light it."

Johnny complied.

Mrs. Dunbar held the cigarette beneath her nostrils, smelled it, then pressed it sideways to her lips. Then she held it somewhat awkwardly between thumb and forefinger. She turned to Johnny. "I'll spend the night here if you'll feel better."

"They wouldn't let you."

"I could stay in the lobby. I can sleep sitting up."

"They wouldn't allow that either, but even if they would, I don't want you to stay, Aunt Lettie. Go on home. But thanks for coming."

"I'll tell your mom and dad. Tomorrow morning."

He nodded. "Okay. Dad came by Saturday. He said she's not so mad now."

"She's not really mad at all. She just wants you to be okay."

"*Her* okay."

"That's right. Everybody would prefer to have things their way."

"Who's 'they'?" Galway said, very lightly.

"Speaking of *them*," Mrs. Galway said, "I'll talk to the nurse, while you talk to the doctor."

"I imagine he's not here now, but I'll see."

"Douglas may know something," she said. "Ask him, too."

The nurse, a stocky, gentle-voiced woman in her fifties, thought Johnny had experienced a panic attack. "That's what it appeared to be," she said. "He calmed down so quickly once the doctor was here. His breathing got regular, and he quit trembling. He wanted to know if he got really ill, would his parents be allowed to come in. And when Dr. Woods told him no, the rapid breathing started all over. He's afraid."

"So the doctor's not testing the food?" Mrs. Dunbar asked.

"Not now. He might if things changed."

"Could I take it with me?"

"Oh no," the nurse shook her head. "That's impossible."

"Could I take a piece of the candy or a cookie?"

"I don't think so. No. Why?"

"I'm his aunt," Mrs. Dunbar said. "If someone's poisoning him, I want to know."

"Well . . ." Then, "I'm sorry. No. I mean, it may be evidence. I have to keep it here until somebody tells me otherwise."

Mrs. Dunbar had hoped for a different response, but it was the answer she herself would have given.

"He does get afraid," she said to the nurse. "He needs a little comforting."

"We can tell."

Galway had learned a little more than Mrs. Dunbar. Douglas, garnering information from guards involved in transferring Johnny to the infirmary, knew Johnny had vomited in his cell at least once, maybe twice, had had difficulty breathing, and had briefly been unable to walk.

"When they brought him up here," Douglas said, "he told me if he died to tell his parents he had not killed anybody."

In the car again, when Galway passed this information to Mrs. Dunbar, she exclaimed, "See? See? That proves he didn't do it."

"I think so, too," Galway said. "It was worth the trip here."

"I don't know about that. He's so afraid. And he's truly sick, for whatever reason."

"He's not seriously ill, though."

"Probably not in any traditional sense."

"What does that mean?"

"Feeling sick can be serious, Galway. You should know that. Besides, he may have cause."

"How so?"

"I think his mother put something in the cookies, and maybe in the cigarettes and gum, too, that is supposed to fill him with sweetness and light, and flush out all piss and vinegar."

"What?"

"You know. Bad boy stuff."

"Yeah. I guess I know. Piss and vinegar. I'd heard of those. But I didn't expect to hear the words from you—not the first one." He laughed. "How about breakfast?" he said. "Let's start the day over."

She shook her head. "Let's go home."

The rain slid in loose waves over the windshield and Galway turned on the wiper momentarily. The sun was rising, and the droplets sparkled. Mrs. Dunbar opened her purse and took out the cigarette. She held it again between thumb and forefinger. "This *is* a little comforting," she said. "Just the action. Doing something."

Galway understood.

"I'll need to talk with Leroy again, I imagine," he said. "I don't know why he would set Johnny up, but he did. Johnny's hesitation gave that away."

"Johnny has some gumption, doesn't he?"

"It's misguided loyalty."

"Yes. But it *is* loyalty. That's a good start."

"Maybe I'll talk with Beth Wellington first."

"Why?"

"Because I suspect Johnny would be even more loyal to a woman than to a man and I don't want to jump the gun."

The rain seemed to stop for just a second or two, then plummeted again.

"Maybe you're right," Mrs. Dunbar said. "And that might be a good trait, too. At least it's normal."

* * *

In her home, Mrs. Dunbar put two napkins on her kitchen table. On one she penned G—the ballpoint wouldn't glide enough for a whole name—and on the other J. On each napkin she placed a cigarette. One had come from Galway's pack, and one from the shirt she assumed was Johnny's. It had been on the hospital chair. Even without close examination, she could see the cigarette from Johnny's shirt had a looser tobacco. When she lifted the cigarette, she saw a faint reddish line on the napkin. She doubted that was normal. She considered phoning Galway, but didn't. The sun was rising, she was tired and excited too, and this was her own little investigation. She would tell Galway soon enough. She wished she knew something about herbs and poison, really *knew* it.

* * *

Galway warmed up some strong, left-over coffee, and sat down at his kitchen table. The murderer could be any of them. Maybe Beth. Maybe Earl. Even Anne. One of the other musicians. The bartender. A stranger.

He got another pack of cigarettes from the carton, but didn't open it. Maybe he wouldn't. His father had been a pipe smoker for years, then gave it up, but carried one around a few more years. And died from a faulty heater. Just like that. His mother and father had both died in one night, still healthy, going to sleep, dreaming, filled with a future, yet never waking up again. Never again.

He couldn't bear the thought, the fact. There was another matter at hand, immediate. He grasped it. The murderer wasn't a stranger. No, that wouldn't do. It was one of the circle, Galway was sure. Which one would let someone else take the blame? It was a despicable trait. He thought of a more significant question—who knew of the crawl space entrance?

What if they all did?

~10~

Devil Do

MONDAY MORNING, WHILE ANDY TRACED DOWN, BY PHONE, Dr. Wood's report on Johnny Rowland, Galway relaxed in a deeply cushioned leather chair. Andy liked nice things, new ones and old. The tables in his office displayed ancient books, opened to interesting outmoded laws. The walls were filled with photographs of old courtrooms, documents, and people, some of them famous attorneys or judges. One photo differed. It was of a young man with an elfin smile and a thatch of thick, straight and wild black hair. He was shirtless, on the deck of a dilapidated fishing boat, with a very small boy next to him, also shirtless, also with an elfin smile. The man was Andy's grandfather, the boy, Andy's father.

"They're not going to run any tests because Johnny's okay," Andy reported. "He's back in his cell. As for the mysterious visitor, it wasn't a girl. It was Earl Wellington."

"I'll be damned."

Galway thought of Earl's friendly nature. Earl would visit a friend in jail, just out of kindness alone. But what had transpired between the two?

"I'll see what I can find out," he said.

"Remember to push," Andy said. "You can be as gentle as you wish, but don't stop too soon. Don't digress to the point you forget what you're after."

"You don't know my methods as well as you think," Galway said.

"Yes, I do. Be as devious with others as you are with me."

"Ours is a game," Galway said. "The stakes differ."

* * *

Galway dropped by the Musicians' Arte. Earl was seated on a high, wooden stool, tuning a banjo for a boy eagerly watching.

"In a minute," Earl said. "This is one of my few talents." He plucked the strings, made another twist or two, and handed the banjo to the boy, who, with a shy nod toward Galway, left the shop. Earl pushed the stool toward Galway and brought another from behind the counter.

"It's easier to talk to you if we're closer to the same level."

"I thought you didn't play," Galway said,

"I don't. But I can tune anything with strings, if I know how it's supposed to sound."

"You visited Johnny, I hear."

"I did. I felt like I should. He's in the loop, you know. One of us."

"No, I didn't know. I thought he just hung around."

"He's a regular in his own way. He'll help anyone. And he's a good audience."

"Did you take him anything? Books? Food?"

"I didn't know I could take anything in. It's my first time even going to a jail. I'm sorry he's in there. If I go again, which I don't plan on, I'll take him a"—he turned, still sitting on the stool, to glance at the display case—"a penny whistle or a recorder."

"I doubt they would be allowed."

"They could be fashioned into a weapon, huh? Johnny might be good at that. He can fix things."

"They're also concerned that he could injure himself, which I suspect is more likely. What did you and Johnny talk about?"

"Didn't he tell you?"

"I need to hear it from you, too."

"Testing us?"

"I guess."

"We didn't really talk about anything at all. He was embarrassed, I think, for me to see him there. I'd probably feel the same way. I told him that we're all sorry he's in trouble, and we hope he's out fast. He said he doubted he'd be out as fast as he wanted. That's about it."

"Someone suggested to Johnny that he steal from Luke Michaels. Did you know about that?"

His soft grunt could have been from surprise or approval. "Johnny didn't have to go along with it, no matter who suggested it. People say things." He stood up, scooted the stool to the side of the room.

Galway gestured at the wound on Earl's hand. "What happened there?"

"A fiddle string. I was tuning my sister's fiddle, holding it backward, so if the string broke, it wouldn't get me. Well, it popped from the bottom end and curled up and over the neck and stuck right into me. The end was jagged wire. I had to almost rip it out. I heard of a guy who got blinded by a broken string. I'm lucky." He touched the wound gingerly. "It's little, but it hurt like hell." His expression didn't match his conversation. He was patient with Galway but very tired of him, too. He was an unhappy young man.

Galway left the shop and walked down the sidewalk. The street was losing its charm. There was a sordidness to this whole community. He felt as if he had stumbled into a maze, where talented people got trapped. But maybe that was an ugly illusion created by Luke's death, or maybe by Luke's earlier presence, his influence. Maybe these young people would recoup, become excited about the future and themselves. Bad times came and went. A person had to take a deep breath and a bold step. A young woman admiring his BMW shifted her attention to him as he approached.

He winked and she turned away. He glanced up as he unlocked the door. She had looked back. She smiled.

It lightened his mood.

He had, still, to talk with Beth Wellington. He switched on the CD player, then changed his mind, and turned it off. Music clouded issues sometimes. He took a cigarette from the pack, but didn't light it for two blocks.

* * *

Beth Wellington had two jobs, Galway learned, in addition to her band's gigs. Neither job could have paid much. She was a part-time waitress at two local cafes, fitting her hours around her employers' needs and her performances. Monday afternoon she was at Half Beat, a tiny shot-gun restaurant, so narrow it could have originally been an alley between the beauty shop and dance studio. Just inside the entrance the breadth allowed three small tables on each side of the door. The remaining length of the room was divided between an order counter, high stools, and a single row of tables. The immediate impression of the place was coolness, first from excellent refrigeration, rare in this town, and second from the extensive amount of chrome, on tables, chairs, counter, and picture frames. But an odd charm asserted itself quickly. Paintings by local artists and photographs of their works were displayed on all available wall space, a unique and unsettling mixture of colors and textures.

Beth left a rear table to lean her guitar against the wall.

"Hey," she said.

"I'm the only customer, huh?"

"We get some of the college crowd. They're in early and late."

"You entertain here, too?" He nodded at the guitar.

"I practice when nobody's here. Sometimes other people pick it up."

She was dressed for a performance, Galway thought, or maybe for making tips—if college kids tipped. She wore black cotton slacks and matching laced-up vest, no blouse. The lacing was tight, modest and provocative simultaneously. A silver headband graced her wide brow, was almost hidden in the back by wildly curly hair. He suspected the curl was natural. A silver chain encircled her tiny waist, then drooped down, forming a loop over her right thigh. Her short nails were shades of brown and wine, colors repeated in her eye shadows. He smiled in spite of his determination to be professional and straight-forward and knew she could read his smile.

He took a menu from a stack on the counter. Hand-printed on the backside of a flyer for the Musicians' Arte, it listed four kinds of bread, six kinds of cheese, humus, alfalfa sprouts, bean sprouts, spinach, red onions, brownies, cheesecake, coffees and teas. A lopsided star marked a raspberry float special.

"I'll try that raspberry float," Galway said.

"Pick a table." She walked behind the counter.

He watched her instead. The makeup might be artifice, but she would be lovely with no artifice, perhaps more beautiful than with it. She was one of those women who would be beautiful in any era and any setting.

She placed the float and a napkin on the counter top and put her hands on her hips. "Two seventy-five."

He laid a five by the glass. "Keep the change."

She nodded.

"I came by to talk to you," he said. "Do you have a few minutes?"

"About what?"

"Luke Michaels."

"I guess so, just until people start coming in."

She joined him at the table near her guitar.

"I'm not singling you out," he said. "I've met with Anne, Leroy, Luke's partners, Hank and Merle, and I just finished talking with your brother."

"Did Earl send you here?"

"No."

"I didn't think so." She crossed her forearms on the tabletop edge, leaned forward. The movement seemed absolutely natural, but it was also provocative, lifting her shoulders and accenting the fullness of her breasts. "Why do you want to know about Luke? You're not a cop. And you probably get the same story about him they got. He was an asshole, which everybody knew. I know Earl told you that the first time you talked."

Coming from her, the crude description of Luke was jarring. Galway felt slightly embarrassed for her. "In so many words, yes. And so have other people. But I think you might have known Luke better than some of the others did."

"What makes you think that?"

"He took some of your songs. I found them in one of his journals."

She didn't seem surprised. Galway assumed she knew about the journals, but he continued as though it were new information for her.

"Luke had a method," Galway said, "of claiming works. He kept blank pages in his journals, and when he found something he liked, he antedated it. He wrote it in his journal under a date far earlier than the actual author composed it. One of your pieces, for example, he had dated in February five years ago."

"He wasn't even here five years ago."

"Exactly. As far as his records show, he wrote 'Long Goodbye' while he lived in Chicago, before he met you. At least, I assume that was before he met you."

"Five years ago? I was seventeen and—believe it or not—an honor student at Willmore High. Her black eyes swept over Galway briefly. "I always did well in school."

"I believe you'd do well in just about anything."

She was a little flustered. She dipped her head slightly. "Thank you."

"You're welcome."

"I've written better songs than 'Long Goodbye.'"

"I'm sure you have. 'Devil Do' isn't in the journals I've seen. Neither is 'Desert Night Sky Waltz.'"

"You know those?"

"I heard you at the Boondocks, remember? And I have your CDs. I have three of them, at least. Are there more?"

She shook her head. "No. But I have new songs. They're just not recorded yet, not in any finished way."

"I'd like to hear them. Anything you sing has to be good. But, returning to Luke. Some of your songs *are* in his journals, in bits and pieces, single lines, half a stanza. I'm sure more will show up in journals that are missing now. He had also taken lyrics, and probably melodies, from Leroy, Anne, and Earl. He may have taken lyrics from musicians all over the country. I don't know. He's been at this a long time."

"He had Earl's songs, too?"

On her, frowning was a beautiful expression. "Yes," he said.

"How do you know they were Earl's?"

"I read the credits on your CDs. You listed your brother."

She seemed to reassess his features. "Do you always read labels?" Her voice had softened. He wondered why. "Yep. And inserts."

"Are you a musician?"

Galway chuckled. "No."

"Earl is, but he doesn't know that. He thinks a voice alone doesn't count."

"We both know that's not true."

"He has no confidence."

"He has confidence in you."

"I know." She moistened her lips, sighed. "How's Johnny?"

The question seemed out of context, though he expected it eventually. "He's scared and trying to be heroic. You know him pretty well?"

"No. But he's a nice kid. Everybody likes him."

"Isn't he about your age?"

"I guess so. But he's still younger than I am."

She did seem mature, more Galway's age than her brother's.

"Okay," she said, hands in her lap. "What do you want to know?"

He wasn't quite ready for the shift. "Bluntly, were you in the house the night Luke Michaels was killed?"

She nodded.

He was astonished. So quickly, easily, no evasion. "Who was with you?"

"You already know, don't you?"

"Leroy?"

"See?" she said. "You don't need me to tell you anything." She folded a napkin, folded it again.

"Yes I do. I need to know exactly what happened, in as many details as you can recall."

"Okay," in that soft, husky voice.

"Are you comfortable talking here? We could go to Andy's office."

"Who's Andy?"

"Johnny's attorney. Andy Fielding."

"Do I have to talk to him?"

"No. At least, not right now."

"If I leave here, I have to close up. This is my shift. They don't do much business."

"Whatever you say. Are you okay?"

"Yeah. I'm fine." She unfolded the napkin, smoothed it flat as she spoke. "I've been wanting to tell somebody about it. I *should* have. Wanting to doesn't count, though, does it?" She looked up at him.

"It counts with me," he said.

"Okay," she said. "I was supposed to meet Luke when we finished

134

at Boondocks. But I didn't want Earl to know, so I left after my set, while Luke was still playing."

"This was the night he was killed?"

She nodded. "Saturday. A week ago. Sometimes Earl and I ride together, but I had taken my car so I could leave when I wanted. Earl often stays until the end, to be an audience for anybody on stage. About eleven, I went home, left my stuff," she glanced at the guitar, "and took a cab to Luke's. That way, if Earl came by, he'd see my car and not come in. He wouldn't wake me. He knows with two jobs, I don't get much rest."

"Why didn't you want Earl to know?"

"That's pretty obvious isn't it? For one thing, he's my brother. He didn't care for Luke. He thought I was sinking pretty low. He was right. He usually is."

"How did you get in Luke's house?"

"I had a key. Maybe every woman Luke knows has a key. Maybe there are four hundred and thirty-two keys floating around in female hands."

"That's no strike against you, Beth."

"Yes, it is. Anyhow. I just waited, in the living room, in the dark. After a while, I undressed, partly. Not completely. Luke likes. . . You don't need to know that. Someone was in the house." She paused, evidently assessing Galway's knowledge of this. He nodded. It was what he had assumed. She continued. "But I thought I was alone. I waited maybe half an hour, maybe more, and heard a car. Someone dropped Luke off."

A young fellow dressed in a dark blue suit with a sharply red tie came in. His flushed face and damp temples and forehead indicated he had been in the heat for some time, but he didn't remove his jacket.

Beth gathered his napkin and empty glass. "Just a minute, sir," she said, in the direction of the customer. She went into an adjacent room and came back a couple of minutes later, smudges gone, pastels gone. The silver headband remained.

After placing his order, the customer bobbed his head toward Galway but returned to the front table and sat facing the window.

When Beth joined Galway again, she brought iced drinks and napkins for them both.

"What's this?" He sipped it. It had a woody taste.

"It's supposed to be calming," she said.

"Every woman believes that about tea."

She smiled weakly. "Because it's true. About some teas, at least."

Her black eyes were flecked with silver, like fragments of sunlight. She seemed less anxious. She wanted to tell the story.

"I needed," she said, "to tell Luke something. I wanted him in a good mood, and I thought he was. He said I looked beautiful. He wasn't much for complimenting. He loved pretty words, but he didn't *use* them. I thought he was glad to see me. That didn't last long." She played with her glass. "I told Luke I'm pregnant." She looked at Galway. "He said, 'that's too bad.'"

"Nice guy."

"Yes. He never had much emotion. That's worse. Luke told me to go on home. He said he wasn't interested anymore. I didn't know what to do. Who acts that way? Bye babe. Get along darling. I put my clothes on and he watched. I could have been a bird. Then he went down the hall, finished with me. I followed him. I heard him yell something. I thought it was at me. When I got to the door, someone was coming out of the closet and Luke was grabbing him. I didn't know what was happening."

"Leroy surprised Luke, or vice versa."

"Leroy was holding him from behind, but Luke had a knife and was twisting like crazy. Luke stabbed him. I didn't know how bad. Leroy twisted Luke's arm down, and the knife got turned into Luke. They kept struggling, Leroy hit Luke pretty hard, and the knife wound up on the floor, at my feet. I got it. I had to do something.

"You stabbed Luke?"

"It wasn't deliberate. I had the knife, and he fell forward, sort of toward me, and I jerked it up. It got him . . ." She touched her throat. "Somewhere here. Maybe twice. It was all a blur."

"In the throat?"

"Yeah."

"You said 'maybe twice.' Could it have been more?"

She thought. "No. Maybe once. Twice. But not more."

"Okay. Go on. What happened then?"

"We left. Leroy said we should call the police, but then he changed his mind."

"Where was Luke?"

"On the floor."

"Where on the floor? By the bed? Under it? Near the door?"

"At the foot of the bed, I think."

"Was he moving, talking?"

"No. Well, maybe he was moving. You mean was he alive? Yeah, he was alive. I'm sure he was. We couldn't have hurt him that bad."

"Okay. Go on. Tell me how you left."

"What do you mean how?"

"Which door?"

"No door. Under the house."

So she was telling the truth. "Under the house?"

"There's a hole in the bedroom floor, under the dresser. That's how Leroy got in. He took me out that way."

"Did you take anything with you?"

She frowned. "No. What would we take?"

"You tell me."

"Oh. You mean the journals. Maybe Leroy took one. I don't remember."

"Who left first?"

"I did, sort of. I went down the hole first, but I was afraid to crawl out and I didn't know which way to go."

"Where did you leave the knife?"

"I had it with me. I guess I dropped it. It's somewhere under the house."

"Did you take anything else with you?"

She folded her napkin. "No"

The other diner had finished and now stood at the door, smiling toward Beth and apparently bracing himself for another searing walk outside.

"Come again," she called. Then, to Galway, "He's a regular. He's the music theory professor on campus. He publishes reviews of books about music. He'd probably laugh at our music."

"I doubt he'd laugh if you were around."

"He always wears a suit. He says it's the least he can do for his students and for the atmosphere of this pleasant little town."

"Good attitude."

"Yes, it is."

She seemed through with their former discussion. And so calm. Galway guided her back.

"Tell me how you got away from the neighborhood."

"I told you. Under the house. We crawled out and ran across the back yards to the sidewalk."

Galway stayed silent, in case she remembered anything else. He couldn't quite get a grasp on her nature, but he enjoyed simply looking at her. Flawless skin, the color of rich cream, nails, delicately arched. When she lowered her eyelids, her lashes cast shadows on the paler skin beneath her eyes.

"Did you and Leroy agree to keep quiet?"

"No."

"You haven't talked it over, how to handle questions?"

"No. We haven't talked about it at all. He went home, I went home. I think we've been waiting for someone to tell us what to do."

"Luke had been stabbed four times, Beth."

Her eyes widened. "What? He couldn't have been. Well . . . maybe . . . were they little cuts? When he fought Leroy . . ."

"No. They weren't little cuts. He had two stomach wounds, each made with a different knife, and one of them far deeper than the other."

She shook her head. "Not while we were there. I saw what happened. There was the one knife. It was little, a pocket knife."

"There was another one."

"You're scaring me."

"I'm sorry. But it's a scary situation."

She stood. "I'm going to the police."

"Wait a minute. That's a good instinct but it's probably not a good idea right now. I'd like you to talk with Andy Fielding first. It gets harder to talk freely once the prosecuting attorney has control of a witness."

At the word "prosecuting," her eyes had briefly closed.

"I want to see Earl before I do anything."

"Why?"

"I don't want him to hear about it from someone else."

"Okay. I'll go with you."

"No. I'm not going to run away. I didn't even have to tell you anything. I wanted to. And I want to go to the police, or your friend, or whoever. But Earl won't ever understand why I didn't tell him. I have to do that."

Galway doubted anyone could have refused her. And where was the harm?

"All right. We can meet with Andy in the morning, probably at eight or nine. You should have an attorney before you talk to the police."

"I thought you were an attorney."

"I was. Am. But I'm not good enough for you."

She smiled.

He handed her one of his handyman cards. "The phone number's right," he said. "Ignore the rest."

He went outside, the heat clinging and sultry, and was drawn to head home. But that also wasn't proper in the situation. There were good hours of work left. There was also Leroy, with whom he should talk immediately.

~11~

Crawl Space

GALWAY REACHED THE LOFT AT 3:15, TO FIND THE DOOR LOCKED, and Leroy gone. He found him two short blocks away, walking home. Even his gait bespoke self-assurance. Galway parked the BMW, ran after Leroy, and fell in beside him.

"Beth just told me what happened last Saturday," Galway said. "I thought you might want to give me your version."

"What'd she tell you?"

"Everyone wants to know what everyone else said. I need to know if the stories match."

"So do the rest of us."

"True. True. Okay." Galway stopped walking, and was relieved that Leroy did, too. He probably wanted to confess everything. He just needed a good enough reason. "How's this to start our conversation: Beth didn't enter Luke's house with you, but she exited with you, via the crawl space. She also said you wanted to call the police, and she stopped you from doing that. Enough?"

Leroy motioned to the park area a few yards back. "Let's sit there."

Galway rarely walked with anyone who was near his own height. It was a little disconcerting, but also pleasing, like encountering a race to which he belonged.

They took one of the brick paths radiating from the central court of the park.

"She didn't like the crawl space," Leroy said. "I didn't either. It was different leaving than coming, I'll tell you that. It was like we were under the house in more ways than one. We wouldn't be able to get out. It may still be true, in a different way."

They sat down on a wrought-iron bench. A sparrow lighted nearby, then another, then a robin.

"I guess people feed them," Galway said.

"Maybe accidentally. It gets pretty junky here on the weekends." Leroy leaned forward, elbows on knees. "Where should I start?"

"Why were you there?"

"Do you know about Luke's black books?" Leroy asked.

Galway nodded. "I've read most of them. I guess you have a couple?"

Leroy raised his index finger. "One. You know how they're set up?"

"Yes. They're supposedly chronological."

"Supposedly is right. I thought I'd find my song in the last couple of books, and maybe find one or two more. Then I could show an attorney what Luke was doing. I've kept some records of my own compositions—different versions. I don't throw away drafts. But I can't prove when I wrote them. Of course, Luke couldn't have either. I guess he picked them up at jam sessions. We used to trade off, you know, round-robin choice. He's got a good memory for lyrics. Anyhow, I thought maybe I could prove what he was doing. It didn't pan out."

"Why did you choose Saturday night?"

"Our set—the Keynotes' set—ended at ten. That's early for us, but Kenny had to perform live on the local station, and he needed time to get there, set up and warm up."

Galway remembered Kenny, the pony-tailed, balding fellow. "He's good."

"His whole family is. Last Saturday, he was performing with his mother. They've performed everywhere. She plays, too. She has a beautiful voice."

"So you were finished at ten?"

"Yeah. Anne gave me a ride to my place. I knew she'd go back to the bar. She wants to stay till everyone's played. When she left, I changed clothes, and jogged over to Luke's. I got in the house and went for the journals. That's all I wanted. I had a flashlight. It didn't take long to know I wasn't going to find my lyrics as easily as I had believed. I looked in three or four books and didn't find any of my work."

"But you found lyrics by someone other than Luke?"

"I recognized a few phrases."

"Whose?"

"I'd rather not say."

"Okay."

"I heard someone coming in. I headed for the crawl space, but then I heard a voice, and I knew it wasn't Luke. It was a woman."

"Why would that stop you?"

"I thought it was Anne."

That wasn't, Galway thought, an easy thing to admit to. "I see."

"I just waited. A little while later I heard her messing with the keyboard and I knew it wasn't Anne. Anne's got a light touch, real nice. I was going to get out, then, under the house, and just leave the dresser out of place. Luke would know someone had been in there, but he wouldn't be sure who. Then I got sort of trapped. Luke was in the house and I heard Beth's voice. I heard what she told him. The next thing I knew, he was in the bedroom and coming at me. He's not a big guy, but he's not little either. He had a knife. I grabbed him, just trying to keep the knife away. But holding him was impossible. I think I twisted the knife into him. And he got me, too. Here." He touched his chest just beneath the left collarbone. "I didn't know it until later. I got him to drop the knife." He stopped, sighed. "And we got out of there."

"'We' meaning you and Beth?"

"Yes."

"When did she come in?"

"In the middle of it. I'm not sure exactly."

"Did she get in the fight?"

"Sort of. She picked up the knife when it fell."

"And did what?"

"I don't know. I can't remember the sequence. It seemed to happen all at once."

"Beth says she stabbed Luke."

"Maybe." He leaned forward, elbows on knees, shoulders hunched. "It could have happened when she got the knife."

The movement and change of position allowed Leroy, Galway knew, to hide his reaction. "She says she may have stabbed him more than once."

"Did she say that?" Leroy glanced back, met Galway's gaze briefly, turned away. "Then maybe so."

"Was Luke conscious?"

"He wasn't dead. He groaned. And I think he cursed, though I didn't hear the word. Sounded like a curse."

"Why didn't you call for help?"

He shrugged. "I wasn't thinking."

"Beth said you wanted to call the police."

"Well, I didn't. I thought it might be better to call from somewhere else, after we'd gotten home."

"Why run if he was alive? He knew who you were."

"But maybe he wouldn't have done anything. The knife wasn't that big. I'd been stabbed and I wasn't down. Besides, Beth . . ."

"She wanted to get out right then?"

"She was panicky. I grabbed the book I'd taken and we went out under the house."

"Which direction?"

"West, back behind the corner house."

"And then?"

"We walked, fast, to the intersection. She wanted to go home. I still wanted to call the police."

"Good for you."

"But I didn't. I went home, too. After an hour or more, I rode my bike down to a phone booth and called Luke's number. I didn't want my number on a record. There was no answer. I did the same a short while later. Finally, I called the police."

"Did you talk to Beth?"

"I called her, too, and told her I had phoned the police. We haven't talked since then, except at the Boondocks. She asked me to keep quiet until I had to say something. I think she believed it would all go away." He lifted his hands. "That's it."

"What about Johnny?"

"I would've come forward. There's not a chance he would get blamed for it. He didn't do it."

"The police think he did. He had Luke's blood on his shoes and in his car. He was caught selling some of Luke's equipment."

"I know. I'm really sorry about it." He stood up. "Well, do you have enough?"

Galway stood, too. "Probably, at least for now. Johnny's attorney will want to talk with you. With Beth, too. Separately, I imagine."

"Okay."

"Tomorrow morning all right?"

"As long as I can open the Loft at 11:00." He frowned. "Or will I likely be in jail? Should I make arrangements now for someone else to man the place?"

"Wait until you talk to Andy. I have one more question. Did you set Johnny up to break into Luke's?"

"I'd like to say no. But," he sighed, "I guess I did. I mentioned it to him, even told him how it could be done. But I also told him to forget what I said."

"Exactly what did you tell him?"

"That Luke was asking for a hard lesson, and that a burglar could probably get in through the laundry room window and walk away with a load of electronics. I told him if he went there on Saturday night, while Luke was at the Boondocks, he could get enough equipment to live on for a few months. But in a few minutes, I told him to forget what I'd said, to please forget it entirely, that it was a stupid idea, not worthy of me and an insult and a risk to him, Johnny. It made no sense at all. It was hard, later, to believe he actually did it. I still can't imagine him hurting anyone. Unless he was caught, as I was." He looked at Galway. "Did that happen?"

"According to Johnny's story, no. He never saw Luke at all."

Leroy nodded. "I hope that's true. Even if it's not, I caused what happened. I have to own it all."

"Did you put the blocks under the laundry room window?"

"No. I don't know anything about that."

"Johnny used them to get in the window."

"Oh. No. Like I said, I had let that whole burglary idea go. I was ashamed of it. Still am." He fell silent a moment. Then, "I should never have talked to Johnny. I guess I was thinking of myself as the burglar and him as the decoy. I didn't think far enough ahead. That's how it worked out anyhow. The kind of crazy twist you get caught in." He looked toward the hill beyond the park. "I'd like to go on home, unless I'm supposed to turn myself in right now. Should I go with you?"

"No. I'll call you later tonight with a time to meet Johnny's attorney. I can give you a ride there, too."

"Just give me the time and address."

"Could I give you a ride now? The heat's pretty bad."

"It's cathartic," Leroy said. "Sweating, actual or symbolic, is good for a person." He smiled ruefully. "I am headed for jail, aren't I?"

"Maybe. It depends on what happened in that house."

"I told you. So did Beth."

Galway shook his head. "Neither story accounts for everything."

"What differs?"

"Andy will tell you tomorrow. By the way, we'll need the journal you took."

Galway stayed on the park bench, watching Leroy stride down the brick path, to the intersection, across it, and up the hill. Street traffic around the park had increased, workers on their way home or elsewhere. Galway looked at his hands. The skin was rough. He had nicks and scrapes. One nail was blackening from a poorly wielded hammer.

He wondered, too late, why the dresser was in place if Leroy had left the trapdoor open. He might be able to conjecture an answer to that question.

He wanted to go home, which made him feel callous and lazy. He should stay on the trail in this case, check and crosscheck the stories, until he had answered all his questions or found other avenues to explore. He should be on the trail for hours. He should talk with Anne Mercer again, and Johnny, all the while with new information in his pocket. Leroy's information. He should be *dogging* people. Cases were solved by lab work and leg work, not yard work. But he had had enough. He was tired. And it was true that the tired mind made mistakes. He should clear his thoughts, and let them come together in new ways. That process couldn't be seen, but it most definitely was part of discovery. That was one reason to give himself a break. Another was that he trusted most people to keep their word. He trusted that after he made arrangements with Andy and advised Leroy and Beth, both of the latter would appear at Andy's office at the scheduled meeting. Meanwhile, his remaining questions would order themselves effectively. This was the time to let his work come together.

He went home. He donned jeans, blue shirt, and tennis shoes. He mowed his own yard, then Mrs. Dunbar's, working from the outside in, ever narrower. He liked the closeness of the two residences, as if he and she were remaining members of an extended family. The houses encouraged that illusion, since hers was a duplicate of his, only much smaller. Victorian style, each two-storied, white, with a black roof sharply angled and broken with pitched dormer windows, a deep front porch with a graceful railing, and a lawn green from much rain and much sun. The day Galway had toured the large house, the realtor talking in a chirpy, little girl voice, he had thought the smaller one seemed an important adjunct, as if the long ago families had been related, at least in function, perhaps master and servant. The thought had made him briefly uneasy, since he didn't believe in servitude of any kind. There was no servitude involved in the present relationship. He mowed her lawn because he wanted to. She paid him with food, because she wanted to.

He had expected her home by the time he finished. When she wasn't, he called Andy to arrange a meeting with Beth and Leroy.

"I hope you're right," Andy said, "and we see them both in the morning. If they take off, we're going to hear about this. And pay for it."

"Why would they tell the truth voluntarily and then take off? It doesn't make sense."

"*If* they're telling the truth."

"They are. Leroy was waiting for Beth to make the first move. And she's more concerned about her brother than herself. You'll find out tomorrow."

"You want to come over for some conversation and dinner?"

"No. I need to fix something."

"What's that mean?"

"I'm making a table."

"You're righting the world with work?"

"Yep."

"You want some good news? There's not a trace of Johnny on any of the items under the house. Not even a piece of his wiry red hair."

"Have you talked with him today?"

"Yes. He wants me to give the information to his mother in person. Have you met her?"

"No. But I've heard she's very sensitive."

"Johnny called it 'edgy,' 'extremely edgy.'"

Galway hung up the phone, then went out front and sat on the top step of his porch. He remembered Beth's anxious tone when she said her brother's name. And her worried eyes. Her eyes had large irises, little white. That's what made them so luminous, warm. Her lips were well defined. Everything about her was. He could recall her every movement. Then he remembered the pregnancy.

He got up, whistled a few random notes but they turned into a melody he recognized. Not one of the tunes he'd been studying. No. Older. One his father had hummed. Ah. "The Deil's Awa' Wi' Th' Exciseman." That was it.

He kept whistling, wanted it all to come back to him. Not just all the tune, but every time he heard it, in between and before and after. He wanted to recapture all the memories and encapsulate them in a time bubble and enter it himself. Forever. He didn't want to let go.

12

Finding Yellow

MRS. DUNBAR, EARLIER THAT MONDAY MORNING, HAD NEVER been so aware of the color yellow. Either it was her own fixation or the color had just popped out everywhere today. A tot in the grocery store had worn a yellow print sundress and matching yellow ribbons around two pigtails. A magazine ad displayed rain capes the color of daffodils. A road-side jogger's tank-top was a bright yellow. A taxi. A sports car. A child's wagon—and wagons were supposed to be red! not yellow. Obviously she was supposed to be doing something with that color.

She was home, fixing tea, and choosing a remarkably tiny cup with hand-painted minute flowers, yellow, when the memory finally surfaced—of a special car. She had seen it the day she visited the rector to ask for the videos. The car driven by Miss Miles that day had been yellow and was, if Mrs. Dunbar had her models right, a Ford. But that wasn't Miss Miles' car. At least Mrs. Dunbar hadn't seen it before then. When would she have, given that she didn't go to church every Sunday and usually arrived *after* Betty Miles. But it had most definitely been a yellow car.

Mental connections quickly followed: Miss Miles and Father Madison. His penchant for tiny model cars. Miss Miles and Luke Michaels. Both had fair skin and light, thick hair. Well shaped, graceful people. Not too friendly.

She slipped the cup into its saucer. She held her hands in her lap, mind clicking away. The two were related. No doubt.

With the cup rinsed and on the glistening enamel stove top, waiting for later, she looked up Miss Miles' address in the church directory. Then she freshened her powder, hastily pinned her hair into a thick top-knot, grabbed her purse, and headed for her car.

In a short time, still excited at her possible discovery, she was parking before Miss Miles' house, ignoring a no-parking sign. In the driveway was a green compact car she knew belonged to the choir director. Mrs. Dunbar headed purposefully behind that vehicle and on to the side of the garage away from the house. A small, curtainless window allowed her to peer into the interior. There it was—long and sleek. A car from the past. Yellow.

Surely it was Luke Michaels' car.

She walked back to the driveway, looked at Betty's front door and window. Could she just ask? She saw a shadow behind the front window and waited. When the door didn't open, she thought perhaps she had only imagined the shadow. Oh, she did want to knock. She wanted to pursue this immediately. But she couldn't do it. Not yet.

She drove to a Walgreens and used the pay phone to call Rosie.

Rosie's verbally gifted child reached the phone first and yelled something that sounded like "Hellopened," which, Mrs. Dunbar thought, might be appropriate at the moment. "And hello to you. Get your mommy."

Rosie had already taken over the phone. "I'm sorry about that. Who's calling?"

"It's Letitia Dunbar, Rosie. I'm sorry to call you at home."

"That's all right. You just caught me. I'm on my way to the office. What's wrong?"

"I wondered if I could ask you a few questions about Father Madison and Betty Miles."

"I don't really know anything except what I mentioned Sunday. They've been seeing each other."

"I'm interested in another area. Was she selling him a car?"

"I don't know. Hey, maybe. That would explain some short drives with her."

When Mrs. Dunbar hung up, she called information and got the number for Phil Larsen, who at present was the Vestry chair.

"The Vestry dealings aren't secret, are they?" she asked him.

"They're not supposed to be, but they sometimes are. What's up Letitia?"

"I heard that Father Madison asked for a raise. Is that true?"

"Yes. And he's probably due one. We're going to decide on the amount at the next meeting."

"Is it based on his getting married?"

A brief pause, then, "That hasn't come up, but we wondered. What do you know about it?"

"That he's been seeing Betty Miles very discreetly."

"Not too discreetly, obviously. A marriage wasn't, or isn't, the basis for the raise. If he wants it to be, he could tell us he plans to marry as part of the justification for the increase."

"He probably doesn't want to. He probably wants to have the money before he proposes the union. That way he's bringing her a gift instead of the marriage bringing one to him. And he may feel that he's worth the money by himself."

Mrs. Dunbar waited for his way of thinking to accommodate hers.

In a moment, he said, "Probably."

"Did he mention a car to the Vestry? Buying one?"

"Who told you about that? That wasn't even in the minutes. It's not part of the church business."

"So he *was* buying one?"

"Why do you want to know this, Letitia?"

"Don't I have a right to know it? I'm a member of the church, and we members elect you Vestry. Don't you serve the congregation?"

"Well, put that way, I'm not sure. We're supposed to keep some things confidential."

His tone had changed, and sounded to Mrs. Dunbar somewhat superior. "Then don't tell me," she said. "I can do without your help. I've never had it before." She hung up on him, felt trembly and self-righteous. Her cheeks burned. She walked out of the store, got in her car, rested her forearms against the low curve of the steering wheel, and fumed. She wasn't a nosy person. She had been a member of that church for years and had never asked for an accounting of activity or money. Now, she poses a simple question and Phil acts as if she has pried into the contents of a confessional. Was she in the wrong here? She didn't know and that made her even angrier, only at herself, too.

On the sidewalk beneath the mall awning, a little girl had gotten loose from her mother and was running haphazardly, barely in control of her little body. Her delight in the possible escape showed in her bright eyes and open mouth. Her heart was likely churning with joy. The sight restored Mrs. Dunbar's equilibrium.

She could go back to Betty Miles' home and brazenly knock on the door and pursue the truth. Perhaps that wouldn't even be brazen, just direct and honest, which was the path she most favored. But maybe there was a better direct approach, one suggested by Phil Larsen and his hierarchical reticence. Father Madison. He was the man she thought might be concerned with the car. And he was, by golly, her rector. He was the symbol of truth and liaison with good in this world. He was the person to confront.

She started her car, backed out with a wider swing than she could easily control, and drove off more decorously.

A white card in the passenger seat caught her attention. It was an old library card, fallen from one of the books she had checked out, *Black Arts in the Herbal World.* She turned it over. At the first red light, she put it in the glove compartment. At the second red light, she put it on the dash, print side up, so the sun would hit it, at least every now and then, and burn out any tinge of evil. "Oh," she said, "I'm so ridiculous. I'm getting like Zeena."

Rosie was not at the front desk, but in the children's playroom, wiping down plastic toys with a damp cloth. The room smelled strongly of antiseptic.

"I'll bet you're right about the car," Rosie said, and slipped plastic rings onto their spindle. "This isn't part of my job description," she said, "but if I stuck to the work I'm paid for, a lot of things wouldn't get done."

"Don't we have a janitorial service?"

"Sure. But they don't dust lamp shades or wipe off toys or coffee pots."

"We don't pay you enough."

"I'd like to agree. But it's easy work, and Father Madison lets me pretty well choose my hours."

"When will he be in?"

"Any minute. He's at the gym."

"I'll wait up front, if that's all right."

"Sure. If the phone rings, don't answer it. I'll get it in a second or so."

Mrs. Dunbar chose to wait standing in the rector's office doorway. Across and to her right were the tall bookcases with his miniatures. They had been shifted around. The cars were now on the top shelf, left side, and second shelf, right side, as if they came down a spiral road. The animals were all on the top shelf, right side, and with a new item. From her position, it seemed to be a tree, and a rather large one, with relatively thick branches, two of them lateral and long enough to afford shade, when leafy, to the creatures beneath. It was hand-carved, she was certain, and not finished. On the shelf behind his desk was another tree, or the beginning of one. She wondered if he was starting a village from the outside in, from woods to home. It was a nice thought, little worlds in worlds.

She turned at the sound of the door opening and saw his smiling face. "Letitia!" he said, obviously happy about something. He closed the door. "I've just walked three miles in forty-seven minutes. That may not sound good to you, but it does to me."

"It sounds miraculous to me."

"You're joking, right?"

"Not really. I have no stamina for sustained walking, though I can last for a long time if it's done in short stages on a level surface, no grade."

He motioned her ahead of him into the office, and called "Rosie!"

It was met by "I'm mopping the floor in here."

"Okay! Don't stop! Just wanted you to know I'm back!"

He smiled at Mrs. Dunbar, went around his desk and sat down. "Is it about the videos again?"

"No. I want to ask about something that may be your personal business. And if it is, and you don't want to discuss it with me, I'll leave. I won't be offended either. Phil Larsen just advised me, in so many terms, that Vestry business wasn't my business."

"If he did, he was out of line. The Vestry serves the congregation, not the other way around."

"That's what I told him."

"But they *do* have to keep some things confidential."

"Such as?"

"Suppose you wanted to donate money for perpetual flowers for a friend, and you wanted it to be anonymous."

"Then I'd send a money order or cash, without my name, or

through an attorney. I wouldn't make the Vestry bear the secret for me."

"Good woman! And a good idea. Some people don't do that. They make a bequest or a request and they want it quiet, quiet for decades. Right now, for example, the parishioner who wants the chalices to be pure silver also wants anonymity. The financial outlay would be for the church, not for the person."

"You mean someone in our congregation really won't put his name to his own suggestion?"

"His or *her* name."

"It's all a little too precious for my tastes."

"Between the two of us, maybe I agree. But we're dealing with humans." He sighed, leaned back and swiveled his brown chair a little. "What of my private business do you want to discuss?"

"A yellow car presently in Betty Miles' garage."

He stopped moving the chair.

Mrs. Dunbar hurried on. "I'm sure it belonged to Luke Michaels. I think Betty's a relative of his, and that you're purchasing the car, or want to." She paused. "And that's it."

He nodded, fiddled with a business card at the blotter's edge. "Well, Letitia," he said slowly, "that's a pretty big it. And only part of it is my business and thus mine to tell. I *am* buying a car. I guess I may admit, too, that I'm buying it from Betty Miles. I'll probably get the title in the next day or two. It's a beauty. I guess you know that. But the rest of the information belongs to Betty. I don't know why you're interested."

"You know my nephew's in jail. The police believe he killed Luke."

"Yes, but the car doesn't change that."

"Maybe not. But it's a fact in the story, isn't it? It was parked at his house sometimes. People thought he owned it. And sometimes he drove another car, a green one. I'm sure that's Betty's other car, the one she usually drives. So, he was driving one of her cars most of the time."

"But the cars have nothing to do with his death."

"Even if that's true, the police should know about them."

He laid the card near the phone. "Well, you have a point. I have talked to the police, just this morning. They know about the car."

153

"Why didn't you say so?"

"This is one of those areas where privacy matters."

"Do they know about Betty Miles?"

He didn't answer. Mrs. Dunbar felt sheer exasperation, but also understood his silence. "Never mind," she said. "I know I'm right."

"Look, Letitia." He came around the desk, sat on its corner. "I'm not trying to be secretive. I'm trying to keep confidence, the same as I would for you or anyone. But I have an idea that might help you and help someone else, too. You said you wanted to confront Betty about the car, but didn't, out of respect for her privacy. Maybe she'll want to talk with you. Maybe she needs to talk with someone. Would you be willing to go out there and just be your gracious self? Your kind self?"

"I don't know."

"Give me a minute, okay? Wait out front with Rosie?"

Mrs. Dunbar did so.

Rosie was now behind her own desk. "Well, was he buying a car from Betty Miles?"

"You'll have to ask him," Mrs. Dunbar said, and Rosie lifted her eyebrows. "I'm sorry, Rosie, but I've been chastised. Gently," she added, "but chastised nonetheless."

"You shouldn't pass it on."

In a moment, the inner door opened, and Father Madison stepped out. "The visit is fine, Letitia," he said. "Walk softly. Betty's quite vulnerable right now."

* * *

When Mrs. Dunbar arrived at Betty Miles' house, Betty was waiting on the porch. "I saw you earlier, as you were driving away. It worried me."

"That was unkind of me. I was snooping."

"About the car?"

Mrs. Dunbar nodded. She followed Betty into the house. The living room was tiny, and served as dining room, too, with an oval table before a lovely curved bay window. The window seat held myriad green plants, some healthy and full, others dry with curling leaves.

Betty had moved to the table. "Let's sit here," she said. "In the sun. Father Madison said you know about me and Luke."

"I noticed a resemblance last Sunday, in church, when you stood a certain way. I had seen some photos of your brother at church functions. And in a video. And in church, too, of course."

"With the choir."

"Yes."

"I was a little surprised how much we looked alike with his hair long. He didn't wear it that way back home. So I cut mine short. It was time, anyhow. You know, after a woman is thirty."

"Ignore that old rule. Your hair is lovely. You should wear it however you please."

Betty nodded. "Would you like something to drink? Coffee? Juice?"

"Just water. If it's no trouble."

"Ice?"

"Please."

"I'll be back in a minute."

Mrs. Dunbar glanced around the room. It was very peaceful, white and blue, very neat. A spindle magazine-holder next to a piano held what looked like sheet music. An arched wall-bookcase held hymnals and a few crystal figurines. A larger crystal angel and a wooden metronome shared the piano top.

Betty returned, placed a crocheted coaster before Mrs. Dunbar and set the glass of water in its center. "It's your nephew they've arrested, isn't it?"

"Yes. But he didn't kill your brother. He did steal some things from Luke's house, but he didn't kill him."

"How can you be so sure?"

"I just know Johnny." Mrs. Dunbar saw the hint of resistance in Betty Miles' eyes, and corrected herself. "I could be wrong. I wouldn't want to lie for him."

Betty sat down. "How did you know to look here for the car?"

"Last week, when we met in the church patio, I had already seen the car. I thought the flash of yellow was your dress, but later I realized I had seen the color before I saw you. Then I stumbled upon the rector's fondness for cars. Eventually all the little details came together."

Betty rose to open two windows behind the plants. When she did so, the sound of a high whir, like a bicycle wheel-whistle, came from a distance.

"That's nice," Mrs. Dunbar said.

Betty sat down again. "It's been really hard," she said. "I haven't known what to do. Every decision seemed so selfish. I didn't want to feel certain things or admit to them and I delayed and delayed. There's the problem of people knowing I'm Luke's sister. And the problem, embarrassing as it is, of burying him." She glanced up at Mrs. Dunbar. "I don't have much money. The car I was giving to Luke. I didn't have to. Our dad died a couple of years ago, and I sold everything but the car. It was Dad's baby. I planned to give Luke a choice, the car or money. First he said one, then the other. I ended up buying a used car for transportation. And finally, recently, I decided that I should sell the car and give him the cash. That would be the end of it. You know, he couldn't get himself together. He would have kept the car without caring for it until it lost all its value. I urged him to put up a carport near the house to keep the car out of the weather. I had to pay for the materials, of course. He didn't do it right. He wouldn't do anything—advertise for a buyer, get estimates. Anything. With Luke, nothing was real but music, music, music."

Mrs. Dunbar ventured "I know. I've seen his journals."

"You have? How?"

"An attorney friend asked my opinion." Betty's expression reflected a slight change in attitude. She had been briefly impressed. "But the contents didn't pertain to you," Mrs. Dunbar continued. "They were just lyrics, hundreds of them."

"That sounds like Luke."

"He's always kept such records?"

"Of one kind or another. Luke *always* wrote. When he was little, it was on scraps of paper. He'd stick them in his pocket. He'd leave them in jars or drawers, anything covered. Sometimes the note was personal, like 'you hate me and I know it' or 'I'm going to run away,' but usually it was just a word or a sentence. They didn't make sense."

"Now the notes are poems and songs, saved in bound books, and all written in a beautiful script. Well, actually it's *printing*. But lovely printing."

"He started putting things in books later, and then began rewriting with no errors. He could spend a long time doing that. And a long time listening to music."

"Were the songs his?"

Betty Miles shook her head. "I don't know. I haven't thought about it." She leaned back, turned to look out at the sunny yard. "I told him last Saturday the car was sold. He was excited about the money."

"Saturday? The night he was killed?"

She nodded. "He came here from the bar and I drove him home. I wanted to keep the car out of his hands until the deal was closed. If I'd gone in the house with him, he might be alive." She looked aside. "Or I might be dead. Who knows?"

"Why haven't you gone to the police? You might have seen something that could lead to the killer."

"I didn't see anything, or I would have gone to them."

"It's none of my business, Betty, but don't you wonder who killed him? and why? How can you let it go?"

"I don't want to know any more than I have to. I'd rather not think about it. I'm sorry about him. I'll grieve for him. I mean, I *am* grieving for him. I think I am. But he's been a heartache as long as I can remember. My father got sick trying to deal with him. He would go into rages about Luke, and he wasn't a healthy man. Luke didn't respond to other people. Anger, fear, love—nothing seemed to move him. Nothing but music. He stole whenever he felt like it or thought he needed something. He never took much. He had a kind of limit on his thefts, like a personal code. He took money from my purse, Dad's wallet. He used the ATM card occasionally, wrote bad checks. He sometimes shoplifted. He wouldn't work. Dad changed the locks on the door twice. Luke just broke in through the bedroom window and acted as if nothing had happened. I think Dad was afraid Luke could kill him. I asked Luke to leave, and I borrowed some money to send him out here. I worried he would come back, but he didn't. He liked it here." She drank the remaining water from her glass, shook it as if the cubes were dice, then set it down. She shrugged. "I thought maybe he had changed. Maybe he had found something to keep him in a normal pattern. So when my father died, I drove the car out. I thought I'd see how Luke was . . .

getting along, see if he was stable. I didn't intend to stay. But he seemed so healthy. He was living in a decent rental house, very neat. He was performing with people. He played some of his music for me, and he does . . . did have a good voice. Even when he was little . . . He . . . Well. He was blessed with a good voice. He wasn't blessed with a good nature."

"He was ill, I suspect." Mrs. Dunbar had gathered this.

"Yes. I guess. I'm also afraid of it. Maybe it's in our blood. I'm not crazy and I don't think I'm mean, either. But if people here knew I was his sister, they'd always be looking for the traits to appear. In me and my . . . my kids if I ever have any."

"Does Father Madison know about Luke's history?"

Betty nodded. "Yes."

"He doesn't judge him harshly, does he?"

"No, he doesn't. He says Luke deserves a service. I was going to let the city bury Luke as a pauper, or whatever they do here. But Father Madison is going to claim the body, when it's released, and have a small service. Luke will be cremated. The money for the car will more than pay for that."

"Father Madison's a good man," Mrs. Dunbar said, "and he seems to think well of you." She thought that might be a kind thing to say.

Only when she was outside again did Mrs. Dunbar realize the atmosphere in Betty's home had been oppressive. Open windows and sunlight couldn't transform the past. Betty and her brother lacked a loving bond. Perhaps the father had, too. Such things just happened, with no cause and perhaps with no redress.

Mrs. Dunbar sighed. At least she had found the yellow car. But Johnny was still in jail and a murderer was still loose. She herself was an old woman. How often could a person just stumble on the truth? She started the car. "Maybe," she said aloud, "as long as she keeps looking for it."

13

Rather a Stranger

WHEN MRS. DUNBAR FINALLY DROVE HOME, AFTER-WORK traffic poisoned the air. But the sun danced on the metal trim of cars, and a few birds swirled up from a phone wire as if they were a wave of wings.

She had no sooner parked under her carport than she heard a distant slap which she recognized as Galway's rear screen door.

She walked around back to wait for him, and there he came, long, lanky strides across the side yard they shared. "Have I got news for you," he said. "Some of it very good."

"About Johnny?"

"Yep." They walked toward her steps. "There's not a trace of his blood or prints on the pocket knife or on the rug they took from under the house. They haven't found the other knife yet. But—the bad news—Beth and Leroy were involved."

"Not Leroy," she said. "I hate to hear that."

"It may not be as bad as it sounds." He followed her into the kitchen and into the living room, sat in a sturdy, high-legged chair pulled close to the sofa. "They were defending themselves against Luke's attack, and they injured him in the struggle, accidentally. But they did leave him there." He continued until he had recapped the facts as told him by Beth and Leroy. As he sketched again the layout of Luke's bedroom, the positions of furniture, doors, people, he moved next to Mrs. Dunbar on the sofa. He noted the Bible on the coffee table. He didn't mention it, though its presence made him wonder if her involvement in the case had made her fearful. She seemed as quick and open as usual, even more so, but small changes in her life were always for a purpose. She wasn't a static person. She acted. Maybe the Bible's presence was because of the murder and her peripheral involvement.

"They could be lying," she said.

"Yes, they could be. I think when people cover for one another, which may be the case here, they can lie more convincingly, because the motive is good. Or so they believe."

"Are you speaking from personal experience?"

"Maybe," he said. He smiled, felt genuine amusement. "Probably."

"I'll bet you were a charming liar," she said, "when you were about five. And maybe later on as well." She put his sketch and pencil down. "I discovered some things today, too," she said. "None of it's as important as what you learned, of course, but it fills some gaps." She leaned forward, slender hands clasped, lips barely containing a smile. She whispered, "I found the car." She raised two fingers in a vee. "Two, really. Two cars."

"How did you do that? When? Where were they?"

"With Luke Michaels' sister. She owns them. I found her first."

"How?"

"It sort of fell to me, like a gift. She's Betty Miles, our choir director. She drove Luke home last Saturday."

"I'll be damned."

"Doubtful, though it could happen."

"What? Oh. Right." He pieced it together, watching her in his mind's eye, Mrs. Dunbar scurrying up steps, across a muddy yard, hunched behind a steering wheel that was nearly as tall as she, her sharp eyes assessing a detail, evaluating a person. Mrs. Dunbar, fearing and fighting.

Galway stood up. "Look, you may not be tired, but I am. Let me take you to dinner, and you tell me everything, just as it happened."

"I have plenty of food here for dinner."

"Let me take you out."

"No."

"Okay. I'll order pizza. How about that? Pizza and salad."

"I can fix the salad."

"Just let me order . . ."

"In return for your mowing my lawn earlier I will make the salad."

"Right. You'll make the salad. I'll order the pizza." He headed for the phone.

When the sun had the reddish tint of last rays, they were again on the back steps, listening to crickets and an occasional bird.

"So," Galway said, "Johnny couldn't have seen more than the headboard and pillows. He couldn't have seen the body or anyone crouched by it."

"But the murderer may not know how much the mirror revealed to Johnny."

"We don't know either. Seeing the person would account for Johnny's concern that the murderer will come after him. Johnny did have blood on his shoes, so he had to get closer than he's admitted."

"Let's think about the rug under the house." Mrs. Dunbar said. "Luke's blood was on it?"

"Yes. On the rug and the knife."

"Let's stay with the rug. If the blood on it came from the struggle with Leroy and Beth, then there might have been no blood on the floor at the foot of the bed, not after the first attack. It was all on the rug."

"That's very possible."

"If Luke were stabbed again before Johnny entered the house, and his body pulled out of sight, the blood might have come from under the bed. If Luke were lying under there, the blood might have flowed just enough for Johnny's shoes to get stained. Johnny would have left a trail without seeing either body or blood."

"All right. The murderer might have seen Johnny, at least as Johnny left. Maybe the fellow raised up."

"Or the woman."

"So," Galway said, "someone came in after Leroy and Beth had gone. The person came through the window, found Luke either unconscious or stunned, and stabbed him again, in the stomach."

"And was still there when Johnny came in the window."

"And deliberately left the way Johnny left."

"Who?"

They watched a rabbit come from behind the blacksmith's old shop. It sniffed, nibbled something, raised up, sniffed, turned and hopped back behind the building.

"I'm afraid I know," Galway said. "But I want to be wrong." He stood up, moved onto the grassy lawn, turned back to face Mrs. Dunbar. "I'd rather it be a stranger. I like everyone I've met. Of course, I might like the stranger, too." He thought about the bookstore owner. "But I wouldn't have to get to know him."

"I don't want it to be Anne."

"What prompted you to think of her?"

"She could've opened the window for Johnny. You said she gave Leroy a ride home from the Boondocks. That means she was available, the house was empty, and she knew what Leroy was doing and when. She probably knew what he had said to Johnny. If not from Leroy, then from Johnny."

Galway whistled. "Good job. She could've come back, too, I suppose, to confront Luke about something." He shook his head. "But I don't think so. Opening the window, though, that's a distinct possibility. And, wait a minute—she could've moved the blocks, too."

"Then maybe she killed Luke. God forbid."

Galway thought of Anne's voice when talking about Leroy, her concern that maybe he had been involved. She had been brave enough to describe Luke's theft and her own duplicity, but not brave enough to place herself in the house the night Luke was killed. Bravery sometimes came in little bits, one step at a time. "I don't think so," he said. "She's a forceful gal, and wants what she wants, but I don't think she's a killer."

"Who, then?"

"Wait until after I meet with Andy tomorrow. Maybe Leroy or Beth will have something new to offer."

"Is it Earl Wellington you suspect? The young man who visited Johnny?"

She obviously didn't want to wait, and she was obviously thinking along the same line he was. "You don't even know him, do you?" Galway asked.

"No."

"Then why would you choose him?"

"Because he visited Johnny for *some* reason, because you said he has a cut on his hand, and because Luke had hurt his sister."

"Somebody should pay you for thinking."

"I don't want to think this way."

"The sister?" Galway asked.

"That would be easier. But no."

"Why would it be easier?"

"Because there's a coldness about her," Mrs. Dunbar said. "She didn't want to acknowledge her brother. She didn't come forward quickly to claim him, to arrange burial. She doesn't even seem to care who killed him. Maybe she's not sorry he's gone."

"Maybe whatever made Luke the way he was shaped her, too."

"Of course. She doesn't *know* she's like him. Or maybe she does, and that's why she held her peace."

"So the sister didn't do it?"

"That would be against nature, but so much is."

They let the subject rest.

Galway ambled home, via the alley stables to see if the rabbit were visible through the cracks in the back wall. Mrs. Dunbar went inside her house and baked almond cookies, dusted with powdered sugar. She didn't know why Galway Evans had befriended her, but she was grateful. It was, perhaps, like having a son. She took a dish of cookies over to his front porch, opened the front door, which he rarely locked, and placed them on the table just inside. A small dish of business cards was there, among them some of his own cards. His handyman card looked familiar, like the one Father Madison had toyed with. But then, many business cards looked alike. How many designs were there?

She returned home, left her front and back doors open to the summer evening breeze. She sat at her kitchen table and took notes from the library books. The witchcraft books bothered her very little now, though when she took a break, she always stacked the herb books atop the others, in case a . . . force . . . could possibly get loose. She had, at Zeena's house, seen bags labeled "pokeweed" "celandine" and "marsyalis." She was going to acquire a bit of each, but not to taste, certainly not. Just to examine, perhaps to smell. At a small mall on the northwest side of town was a store with a formidable stock of herbal concoctions. She had visited there once in order to buy brewer's yeast for popcorn. It was almost as good as salt.

The witch books, she noted, had been checked out so many times that there were three cards in one, and four in another, and two in the third, filled on both sides, and some of the same names appeared. She didn't want to think about that, but who could help it? Perhaps there were witches in this town. Of course, the cards were old, before new systems of tracking. One day they would be thrown away. Or lost. Things had their time and were no more.

A few hours later, before she went to bed, she took the books back to the car and locked its doors. She encountered the rabbit as she returned to the house and said "I hope you're exactly what you look like." She felt a bit of thrill at having said that, as if she had made something possible that hadn't been possible before.

~14~

Quietly Weeping

LEROY CAME TO ANDY'S OFFICE DRESSED FOR A COURT appearance, in a dark blue suit, white shirt, tie, and polished shoes in a shade that could be blue or black. His hair was pulled back severely, held firm by a dark band. He looked clean-cut, clean-minded. His voice, though, had a slight waver, as if he were drawn tight from bone to skin. He had been answering lead-in questions, with Andy establishing a casual friendly atmosphere.

"You really believe Luke was alive after the struggle with you?"

"I know he was. He couldn't have been injured that badly. I would have known. Maybe he was unconscious. Beth says I hit him when he was falling and I jerked free. I could have, I guess. Or he could have hit his head on the bed. It had a wooden footboard." He looked at Galway. "Isn't that right? It's pretty solid wood."

Galway had been instructed by Andy not to supply any answers, but he nodded. He wasn't supplying the answer. He was confirming it. Still, he didn't let Andy into his peripheral vision.

Leroy continued. "Beth was panicked and crying. She said she didn't want to go to jail. She asked me to get her out of there. So I did. I grabbed the journal I'd taken and we beat it."

"Where was Luke lying?"

"Right at my feet. At the foot of the bed."

"On a rug?"

"Yes."

"Which you took with you."

"Beth said it might have my blood on it. Or hers."

"Why would that matter if he was alive?"

"I don't know. We weren't thinking straight. She pulled the rug down with us. We left it there."

Galway interjected, "If you thought he was alive, Leroy, why not go out the door? Why leave through the crawl space?"

"We had less chance of being seen leaving under the house and we didn't want to be seen."

Andy made a note on his legal pad. "You were going to let Johnny be the one who found Luke."

"No, like I told Mr. Evans here, I hadn't even remembered the bit with Johnny. I remembered it later, but not then."

"Then why did you leave the laundry room window open?"

Leroy frowned, glanced at Galway as if to see if the question were a trick. "I didn't. I never left the bedroom."

"The window had been unlocked," Andy said, "and the nail through the frame had been removed."

"Maybe Beth?" Galway offered.

He shook his head. "I don't see how. I didn't hear her go in there before Luke came home, and she couldn't have after he found me. "

"How many times was Luke stabbed during the struggle?"

"Twice, I think. Neither really bad."

"More than twice, Leroy. Try four."

"Whoa." He raised his hands as if calling a halt to the question. "Four? Not a chance. I was there. He didn't get stabbed any four times." He exhaled heavily, as if clearing his head. "It couldn't have been four times."

"Well, it was," Andy said calmly, "and by two different knives. One wound differed, and possibly came later. Can you give a scenario that would explain that?"

"No. I can't even grasp it. It doesn't fit with what happened."

"Not with your story, no. Nor with Beth's. Do you want to change anything?"

He bowed his head, remained silent, obviously recalling the event. "I can't change anything. I told it the way it happened."

"The way you believe it happened," Galway said gently, "and hope it happened, sort of accidentally. You have to entertain other possibilities. Could Beth have stabbed him while you were struggling? or while you were moving the body?"

"I didn't move the body. I told you that. And Beth couldn't have done it. I would have known. I could see her. Besides, she wouldn't do that. I'm sure." He stared at the corner of the desk, then looked up. Could it have been Johnny?" He answered his own question immediately. "No. Forget I said that. I don't believe it was Johnny."

"Neither do we." Andy looked at his notepad. "How did you know about the floor entrance?"

Leroy was concentrating on something else. Galway nudged him. "Leroy."

"I can't figure this out."

"About the floor entrance," Andy said. "How did you know about it?"

"My brother mentioned it. He had a roommate for a while who had lived there. He kept a false drawer. Someone had replaced the drawer with a piece of plywood nailed down. I got to thinking about it. I'd been in Luke's house. I knew pretty well where things were. All I had to do was come up under the dresser. I was buying time to go through the books before Luke noticed they were missing. I thought I might be able to go through a few that night, and take a couple more with me. I hadn't counted on someone coming in early."

"Did you put everything back in place before you and Beth took off?"

"No. What was the point? Luke had seen us."

"You know, it sounds as if you planned a murder."

"Then I would have done it, sir, and I would have closed the trap door as planned."

Good answer, Galway thought. Good for you. "Someone did put the dresser back in place, Leroy. Trap door and dresser."

"From inside?"

"How would you have done it from underneath?"

"I had a piece of rope to loop over the dresser. I could pull it back, slip the rope out. I thought it would work."

"Maybe someone else did that, too. More likely it was done by someone in the room."

"Luke?"

"It could be, if he wasn't hurt too bad. But it could have been whoever came next."

Galway accompanied Leroy to the reception area. Beth had

arrived and was seated in a deep chair with a broad expanse of window behind her. At the sight of Leroy she stood, both hands gripping her purse. "I'm really sorry," she said, very low.

"You couldn't help it," he said.

She looked at Galway. "I couldn't sleep. I wish you'd tell me what's going to happen."

"Ask Andy, after he's talked with you."

"We'll be all right," Leroy said. "Just tell the truth. It's what I did. It's what we should have done from the beginning."

She nodded and glanced toward Andy's office, back to Galway. "You're coming with me, aren't you?"

"Do you want me to?"

"Yes."

"Then I'll do it. Just a minute, though."

He stepped aside with Leroy. "There's no need for you to wait here. You can go about your business until you hear from Andy. I don't know how he'll want to handle all this. It's a jumble. We have to divulge whatever will exonerate Johnny, but I'm not sure how much else we have to provide."

"I keep thinking about that window."

"I can see why," Galway said.

"I may know who opened it," Leroy said.

"So may we. Someone who had a key." Galway didn't need to say Anne.

Leroy smiled half-heartedly at Beth, and turned toward the door.

She wasn't the same Beth in Andy's office. She seemed even smaller, her voice more timid. She wore a pink skirt, a white shell top with lace that lay just under her collarbones, pink headband, and white sandals. Her fingernails and toenails were rose-tinted. The different style didn't disguise her distress. When she said her brother's name, she stopped talking altogether, was near tears.

"So you called him?" Galway urged.

She shook her head. In a moment, she said, "He came by. He had let himself into the apartment, and knew I had gone somewhere. He came back later, after I got home. I wasn't going to tell him anything. I didn't want anybody to know. But I was . . . sort of crazy, I guess. I hadn't changed clothes. I was dirty. I had blood on my hands. I couldn't think, you know? I mean. I had stabbed someone."

"And what did Earl do?"

"I don't know." She said it doubtfully, not meeting Andy's eyes or looking at Galway.

"Yes you do," from Andy.

"No, I don't."

"We'll ask Earl."

She studied her hands. Her voice cracked when she said, "That's what you'll have to do then."

"Beth," Galway said, "you told me yesterday afternoon you wanted to talk with your brother, to prepare him. I assume you did that."

She didn't respond.

"Has he taken off? Were you stalling for him?" When she didn't answer, Galway shrugged, spoke toward Andy. "Well, it seems I messed up."

"I don't know," Andy said. "Give her a few minutes."

She sat with her head down for a while, fumbled in her purse to withdraw a crumpled tissue. When she looked up again, her eyes were still welling and her cheeks were as flushed as if she had rouged them. "He didn't take off. He's at the shop, telling Kenny where everything is."

"He knew you were going to tell us."

"He said 'tell the truth.' Leroy just said the same thing. It isn't easy. The truth isn't easy."

Galway stood. "I'll go after him." He spoke to Andy. "If it's okay with you."

"Sure," Andy said. "He knows you, and he probably expects you."

"I'm going, too." Beth stumbled around the chair.

Twice, as they drove through the light traffic, Beth said, "I hate all this."

"Good," he said. "I hate it for you. And for your brother."

At the Musicians' Arte, Earl was talking with the pony-tailed musician from the Keynotes. Earl acknowledged Galway with a small toss of his head, smiled timorously at his sister, and returned to explaining something.

Kenny seemed distracted now, though, wary of Galway and the situation. "I won't have to do this long," he said to Earl. "You'll be back."

"Beth can help you," Earl said. "She's knows as much about the shop as I do."

With a slow look around the store, Earl went to the end of the counter, took up two black books, the size of Luke Michaels' other journals. He also picked up a harmonica, raised it for Galway to see, then slipped it into his shirt pocket.

"Are you okay?" Beth said as he neared.

"Sure." He slipped his left arm around her waist. "Are you?"

"No," she mumbled. "I'm sick."

Earl got in the back seat, Beth in the passenger seat. Galway started the car and pulled away from the curb.

In a moment, Earl said, "I hope you're headed for the police station. That's where I want to go."

"You don't need to go to the police yet. I'm taking you to an attorney's office, Andy Fielding. He's the one Beth talked to."

"I don't want to talk to him. I want to go to the police station."

"That's not wise. I'd advise you . . ."

"I appreciate your concern. But I don't want to talk with anyone. Just take me to the station, please."

"Look, Earl . . ."

"I can get out and walk there. I should have gone by myself anyhow."

"Okay. Let me represent you. Tell me right now that's all right. I'll call the sheriff. We can shortcut the process a little."

Beth was quietly weeping. Through the rear view mirror, Galway saw Earl lean his head against the window. He had closed his eyes. "I do some legal work," Galway said, "when the case holds personal interest for me."

No answer.

"And I have enough money to post a rather large bail."

He regretted saying that, because he didn't want to sound condescending.

"Thanks," Beth mumbled. "I mean it. Really. We don't have money in my family."

"Maybe not. But you're loaded with talent."

In a moment, Earl said, "I wish the world knew that about Beth."

15

Duty Bound

MID-MORNING, MRS. DUNBAR CAREFULLY REBAGGED THE HERBS she had purchased. She encased each cigarette in plastic wrap, too, and put the small grouping of items into a paisley clutch she used rarely. Then she called Zeena and asked if she could visit.

"Join us for lunch," Zeena said. "Peter will be here and he would like to see you, too."

"Could I come a few minutes early, so I could talk with you alone?"

The delayed "yes" revealed Zeena's reluctance. She might arrange to be gone.

Mrs. Dunbar watered her indoor plants, put the Bible back in the bedroom, on the trunk at the foot of her bed. She changed clothing right before leaving the house, donning a blue and white print dress even though, with her bent back, the front skirt dipped lower than the back. She could disguise her twisted self more easily in slacks, blouses, and carefully selected jackets, but she liked lovely dresses. At times, she even missed them. This one had dark-blue cloth buttons from bodice to hem, a white, wide collar, and quarter-length, white-cuffed, sleeves. Her shoes were dark blue, medium heels, toeless and cut low at the arch. Her feet, she believed, were still attractive and she did like shoes. So did Zeena. Zeena admired good taste and handsomeness. Mrs. Dunbar wanted to set an appropriate tone. They were, after all, a group of people trying to behave well for someone else's benefit.

Today, Zeena wore loose black slacks and a silky, flowing, red blouse. Her short black hair was brushed severely back. She looked like a wiry artist or dancer—and probably was both, Mrs. Dunbar thought, only not professionally so. She *was* talented.

"I've worried ever since you called, Letitia. I thought things were working out for Johnny."

"They may be. This is about Johnny and you."

"Oh." She half turned, as if to leave.

"Don't fly away, Zeena. Please."

A few seconds of apparent doubt, and Zeena chose to stay. "What do you have there?"

Mrs. Dunbar sat down in the dining room, where Zeena's research materials had been. She opened the paisley bag, and placed the contents before her. "Don't be alarmed, dear. Come sit here."

Zeena did so, warily.

"I took a cigarette from Johnny's shirt when we visited him in the infirmary. I have it with me." She pushed the plastic containing that cigarette toward Zeena. "I'm fairly sure it's been doctored with wild indigo and maybe with pokeweed."

Zeena's parted lips and her alert eyes suggested, to Mrs. Dunbar's surprise, interest instead of shame. "How did you know that?" she said, brightly. "I'm amazed."

"I saw the bags on the sideboard, remember? Last week when I visited? They were labeled. I saw 'pokeweed' and 'celandine.'"

"But not wild indigo."

"No. You're right. I found that in a book. It calms the mind."

"It soothes cerebral agitation. That's the exact effect."

"The point, Zeena, is that you sent Johnny cigarettes tainted with wild indigo. And maybe cookies, too. And candy. You poisoned your own son."

"I didn't *poison* him, Letitia."

"What would you call it?"

"Protecting him. Curing him."

"Of what?"

"Everything that's working against him. His addictions—all of them, physical and emotional. Against the influences of others, and against evil in general. Against anything bad coming at him or coming from him. I tried to clean him up, him and the space around him. No habits, no hexes."

"What if your influence is harming him?" Mrs. Dunbar said quietly, knowing full well she risked hurting and alienating Zeena.

Zeena met this with rigid expression and posture, then eased wearily. "There's no end to circles, is there, Lettie?" She pressed her fingertips against her eyes. "The herbs should work against me, too, I suppose, if I was hurting him. At least, I hope they would."

"You just wanted to help him."

"And I have. His attorney told Peter that Johnny might not even go to prison. He may get probation. Now maybe I didn't cause this *completely*, but I *helped*. And I'll bet Johnny is changed, too. I bet he's open to new ideas or maybe sees himself differently, or sees us differently."

"What if he hasn't changed?"

"I'm not going to consider that possibility. That's giving it room in my world and I won't do that." The wide collar of her red blouse slipped, revealing the inner arch of a thin collarbone. She was a tiny, fragile woman, but full of energies.

"Does Peter know about the potions?"

"I don't like that word very much, Lettie. Not aloud, at least. And no, Peter doesn't know about the . . . herbs for Johnny. He knows about them in general. He likes my knowing . . . esoteric information."

Mrs. Dunbar felt a warning flush of apprehension. Her own reality could be changing a little. "I just wanted to verify that it was you who . . . put the herbs in Johnny's food and cigarettes. Because he thought—and I did, too—that someone was trying to kill him. And still, Zeena, even after your explanation, I wonder. He was so very sick. What if he had gotten too much? What if he had eaten it all for some foolish reason? He could have died."

"No, he couldn't have," Zeena insisted. "I used only a touch, and not on everything. And I didn't combine the three herbs even once. I was cautious."

"How could he have gotten so ill from so little?"

"Because he was terrified. Any kind of unusual physical sensation frightens him. It always has. You haven't been in our home enough to know how often he's afraid, and to what terrible degree. And now, Lettie, he *should* be terrified. He's mixed up with the wrong people. Let that cause a physical sensation, even if it's with my help."

"He should feel safe around you and Peter. He should feel that safety in his very bones. You're his parents."

"I do what I can the best I can." A car pulled into the driveway. Zeena stood up. "That's Peter. He's early. Good."

Mrs. Dunbar put the bags back in the clutch, and felt, again, somewhat guilty. When would she stop judging so harshly? Zeena was probably right about herself—she was doing the best she could. Everyone only had so much strength and so many weapons. The world was complex. One fought as one could.

During the following lunch on the patio, she at first felt estranged from Peter, her husband's nephew, but his genuine pleasure at her presence, his warm, deep voice, so much like her husband's, and his concern for Johnny replaced her original fondness for him. So he enjoyed the spice of his wife's eccentricity. Maybe that was understandable. Mrs. Dunbar's own interest was piqued. More and more.

"I have new plans for Johnny," Peter said. "If he gets out of this."

"And what are they?"

"He's good with his hands. I'm going to pay for whatever training he needs that'll let him get a good job in a trade. Maybe he's a carpenter. Maybe he's a mechanic. A friend told me that mechanics may specialize. They can get certified to work on special cars, you know, prestigious cars—Austin Healeys, Bentleys, Mercedes—you name it. I think he'd take pride in that."

Zeena shook her head in a tight, rapid negative. "A mechanic? Don't sell him so short."

"I'm not. I'm opening up to whatever Johnny can be," Peter said. "Let him be the best in his own way. It's better than having him be the worst in our way. If he wants to look and live like a bum, what's the harm, huh? What's the real harm in that?" He took a bite of salmon, studying his wife. When he swallowed, he said, "Well, Zeena? Am I right? Shouldn't we be a little more open here? This is our son."

Mrs. Dunbar had noted the word "open" and knew Zeena hadn't missed it either. Maybe the spell was acting after all.

"What if the training isn't in town?" Zeena asked.

"We'll pay to send him wherever he has to go. We're talking about freedom, following through."

"I don't want him to leave."

With a slightly husky voice, Peter said, "I'm glad to know that." In a moment, he turned his attention to Mrs. Dunbar. "Who was the kid," Peter asked, "who visited Johnny the day I was there? Do you know?"

Mrs. Dunbar realized she *did* know. She had briefly been absorbed only by the situation inside this home. "Earl Wellington, I believe," she said. "You saw him?"

"At the county jail. I heard him mention 'Johnny Rowland' and they gave him the same form to fill out they gave me. He sat down across the room. I didn't have a chance to ask him anything."

"What did he look like?"

"He was a sort of boyish fellow. A little stocky, about five feet seven or eight. He was nervous. He sat by the door. I know he didn't want to be there."

"Did you like him?"

"What do you mean, like him? I just saw him a few minutes."

"Did he seem to be a nice young man, someone you would hire for the store? Did he seem out of place in the jail lobby?"

"I was out of place, I hope."

"That's what I mean. Was he?"

"Yes, actually. He just seemed . . . duty bound."

"Did Johnny say anything about him?"

"I went in first, Lettie. I forgot about the guy until just now, talking about Johnny. Earl Wellington, huh? That's an interesting name. It sounds British. Is it?"

"It could be," Mrs. Dunbar said. "At the very least, it has a nice, healthy sound to it."

Now she was in a hurry to leave. In her car, window down, and her hair loosening more and more from the consequent breeze, she headed for the jail, parking like a veteran visitor. She went inside and asked, through a glass window, of a roly-poly woman in brown, if she could visit Johnny Rowland. She already knew the probable outcome, but trying was her choice. And she had a back-up plan forming—Deputy Douglas, a man who knew how to be kind even when doing his job.

"Are you his attorney?" the woman asked.

"No."

"What's your relationship to Mr. Rowland?"

"I'm his great-aunt."

"The visiting period just ended. The next will be tomorrow morning, eight to eleven."

"Then have him call me right away. He's allowed to do that, isn't he? To telephone whenever he wants?"

"That depends on the guards and what's going on at the time. Why don't you just leave a message?"

"Is Deputy Douglas in the infirmary today?"

"I think so."

"If I could speak with him?"

"Stay right there and I'll see if he can come down."

Mrs. Dunbar moved over by the front window because the air seemed better there and the same space seemed larger. Even though the building was new, it seemed far too old and used. Maybe the function of the place created that atmosphere. The tile floor was unscuffed, but also unwaxed, and appeared dull and trodden. Just outside the door, a tall, cylindrical ashtray was filled with cigarette butts, the white filters sticking up at random, some tipped with bright lipstick. Was lipstick coming back? Had it never left? She turned around, looked at the nearer décor. There were no magazines. The chairs were the standard orange plastic. Two of them had cracked seats. A broken one was by itself, in a corner. Overall, an ugly little part of the world, and now it was part of her experience, now and ever after. Life's participants were ever changing, whether they liked it or not. Zeena wanted a hand in what changes occurred.

"Yes, ma'am" from behind made her turn around. There was the olive skinned, big bulky man who had been kind to Johnny.

"I want to thank you again for being so good to Johnny Rowland."

"I try to be good to everybody."

"I imagine you do."

"Did you need something particular, ma'am?"

"Yes, I do. I really need to talk to Johnny, and I know I can't see him personally, but I wonder if he could phone me right away, just enough time for me to get home."

"We could get him on the office line here, but there'd be people around. They don't have to be within hearing shot, though."

Mrs. Dunbar looked at the woman behind the glass. She assumed there were offices beyond. "No. I'd rather be home if I can't talk to him personally. Could he call me there in say, thirty minutes? And could he have privacy while he's talking?"

"The lines aren't tapped, ma'am. I guarantee you that."

"All right."

"You give me the number and I'll see what I can do." He took a small pad from his shirt pocket, handed it and a pen to Mrs. Dunbar.

She wrote her home number. "Tell him no one is listening. Assure him of that, will you?"

The man nodded. "I will, but he may not believe it."

"I know. He doesn't trust people too much and there's a reason for that."

She hurried outside, and felt immediately that the world was expanding, and especially the space around her. It was such a miracle, freedom. She drove home with confidence. She had been to a jail by herself.

At home, she checked the dial tone of her phone, fixed a pot of coffee, then hovered around the kitchen and living room. Occasionally she went to the window and looked toward Galway's house. He wasn't there. She was glad, though, to know that he lived there and would eventually be home. A sudden thought dismayed her dreadfully—what if he moved away now? What if he became so busy in his own life that he had no time for her at all? That would be normal, wouldn't it? And good for him. But oh! for her. Her life would go back to quiet, empty days, except when she ventured to the library or church or the market.

She wouldn't think on it. She would forge ahead whatever came.

The phone rang and she was right there.

"Hey, Aunt Lettie. I hear you came by. Thanks. You got me a phone privilege."

"I want you to tell me something, hon, you may not want to divulge. But it's really important."

"I don't keep secrets from you."

"I want to know why Earl Wellington came to see you and what he told you. I know he visited. I know he's a nice person."

"What's going on?"

"We know you didn't kill Luke, Johnny. Every little bit of evidence will help prove that and may prove who did."

"What Earl said to me doesn't prove anything."

"Then tell me. Please, Johnny. Help me with this."

Silence. Then, "Okay. Earl said, 'Don't say anything that could hurt Beth.'"

"Do you know something that could hurt Beth?"

"I told you what Earl said, Aunt Lettie. That's all I'm going to say."

She understood. "You're a dear soul, Johnny," she said. "Thank you."

"Bye, Aunt Lettie." He hung up.

She went to the window, her heart racing. Galway was still gone. Should she call Andy Fielding? Should she go looking for Galway? She changed into brown slacks, a pink shirt, and tennis shoes. She put the paisley clutch in the back corner of the spare bedroom closet and went outside. She hosed down the two trees in her street-side yard. She filled a water pan by the alley, there for stray animals. She turned to look at her house from this angle and at Galway's. She turned off the water, went inside, and called Andy Fielding's office. He was gone. She left a message for him and for Galway Evans to call Mrs. Dunbar. It was important. She left the back door open so she would hear the phone, then went looking for the cans of leftover paint in the storage area by the carport. She found a half gallon container with a sludgy blue paint in the bottom. It looked like bad luck to her. She left it where it was. She could buy a new blue, fresh and strong. A pint would probably do.

Planning a project had calmed her. But she wanted Galway to call soon. She knew why Earl had visited Johnny. It was so plain to her.

16

Die for Shame

NEAR DINNERTIME, AT A SERVICE STATION ON THE WAY TO LUKE Michaels' neighborhood, Galway changed into work clothes. He needed physical activity. He headed for Mr. Welker's and the thorn tree. As he drove past Michaels' house, he felt drawn toward it, and why shouldn't he? It was part of his history now, as was Johnny, the Wellingtons, Leroy. And Luke Michaels. A person's past accompanied him all his life. It emerged in brief memories, of scenes, expressions, gestures, scents. Sometimes he lost his place for a moment. Now, he focused on the Welker house, opened the gate, eased it shut, and strode around the house.

Mr. Welker was coming out his back door. "You have a power saw, I suppose?"

"Yes," Galway said, "in the truck. I'm just deciding how to deal with this."

"You cut it down. That's how you deal with it."

"I know. But should I cut off some of the branches first, and get them out of the way? Or would they be easier to cut once the tree was down?"

"You don't want to mess around on a ladder with a power saw," Mr. Welker said.

"I don't need a ladder for some of the trimming."

Mr. Welker laughed. "I guess that's true."

"I thought maybe I'd put in a couple of hours now, and finish the job later in the week. Is that okay?"

"Sure. I'm just happy to get it done. I was thinking about doing it myself, but I'd have to wait until she was shopping or something, and there'd still be hell to pay."

With a sidewalk superintendent, as Mr. Welker was obviously going to be, Galway opted to cut the tree down before trimming.

"Could you put on some goggles," he asked Mr. Welker. "I have only the one pair, and if you're going to help, I'd rather you were as protected as I am."

Mr. Welker was happy to need goggles. He almost scurried into the house. In a few moments, he hurried back, goggles on but pushed up to his forehead. "I can't help lift anything," he muttered. "My wife's watching out the window."

"I'm happy to have a lookout," Galway said. "Keeps me alert. I wouldn't want to fall with this thing."

"I'm pretty handy with one."

"Sorry you can't help me then," Galway said.

"Me, too."

Two hours later, the tree itself down and the limbs sawn into two and three foot lengths, Galway sat on the stump, draping his arms over his knees. His shirt was dark with sweat. Sawdust clung to his clothing and skin. He tried to brush the dust and particles from the backs of his hands and forearms, but gave up. "I think I'm through for the day," he said.

"That's fine," Mr. Welker said. "You've really been going at it."

Galway thought about leaving the saw overnight, but worried about Mr. Welker's handyman heart. He might not be able to resist that temptation. Galway put the saw in the back of his truck.

He rinsed off as well as he could with water from the cooler and a clean rag. Then he removed the blanket protecting the petting table he had made. He ran his hands over the wood, still surprised that it was smooth, that he felt no rough patch, no splinter. It was a three-step table, the top of each step inlaid with honey-colored miniature tiles, easily washable. A small dog could walk up the first two tables and curl on the third. A thick doily or soft towel could make the third level a comfortable napping spot. He carried the piece across the street, whistling a little.

He knocked on the red-haired lady's front door.

She greeted him with a warm "Hello there," while her quick companion yipped and darted and spun.

"I made something for your little guard dog," he said, indicating the table. "If you don't like it, you can give it away."

"You made that for us?" She pushed against the door and he swung it open for her.

He put it by her chair, while the Pomeranian checked his shoes and yipped. "If the dog sits there, you might be able to pet her without much movement."

"I see." She sat down and rested her left hand on the arm of her chair. She smiled up at him. "Why would you do this? It's the kindest thing."

He shrugged. "No, it's not. I just thought of it. You know, an idea comes along and you get caught up in it." The dog, though silent, was still agitated, alternately sitting and standing, trying to look up at Galway. Galway didn't want the table to be useless.

"Maybe she could learn to use it right now," Galway said. "Do you have treats?"

"Do I have treats? On the counter, by the bread box. See that glass jar? Would you get a couple of chews?"

Galway did so, accompanied by an intense Pomeranian. He held one treat near the top tier of the table.

In three light, tiny leaps, the guard dog was in place and was rewarded.

The woman's fingers rested against the gold hair.

It was a nice sight.

Outside again, he glanced at Luke Michaels' house and felt weariness descend as though he had only moments ago seen Earl Wellington, eyes closed against his dark future. The yellow tape was gone. The concrete blocks were still in the yard. Fading sunlight glowed against the outer side of the lattice and turned the crawl space beyond a hazy gray. Galway was uneasy. He got in his truck, exhaled heavily, took a deep breath. This would pass. It was a bad time all the way round. As he drove, he continued to think of Earl, of his statement "I wish the world knew that about Beth." Lyrics, too, rose, as if he were involuntarily looking for something.

"*How still is this night.*"

"*And then, then, perhaps I'll cry.*"

"*Give the Devil his do, Darling.*"

Daring Do lyrics. He felt diminished, as if he had committed a cruel act.

When he drove up the alley behind his house, Galway saw Mrs.

Dunbar waiting for him. He parked quickly, called to her even before he was fully out of the truck. "What's up?"

"I know why Earl Wellington visited Johnny."

"Why?"

"Because he believed Johnny had seen Beth."

Immediately he knew what that implied. Beth had been there when Johnny arrived. And Earl knew it, from intuitively knowing his sister, her expressions, her evasion, but maybe because she told him enough to change the nature of her act or to alleviate her own fear.

Mrs. Dunbar repeated what Earl Wellington had told Johnny:

"Don't say anything that could hurt Beth."

Galway was sick with his own folly, his so-easy acceptance of a lie. Of course. Earl wasn't the murderer. Nothing in Earl's music had an edge of hate or anger, or even power. He just loved and longed.

Only one person had that rising, all consuming passion. It smoldered in her lyrics, her music, and in her eyes.

"Die for shame. Die for shame."

Beth had gone back. First home, maybe to change clothing, to don gloves. She had reentered the house, either with a key or through the laundry window—she could have opened it before she followed Luke into the bedroom and joined the struggle with Leroy. She had returned precisely to find Luke while he was still stunned, perhaps even unconscious. She had come precisely to kill him. Maybe she had been the recipient of Johnny's confidence, his planned burglary. If Luke had not spurned her, she could have warned Johnny away. As it was, she met Johnny's arrival with a crime he would stumble into. She had pushed the dresser back to the wall, pulled Luke's body out of sight, and had hidden somewhere, under the bed or in the closet. She was there while he stood at the foot of the bed, scared, sensing more than he saw. When he left, and finally drove away, she exited the house as he had. His trail led to and from *her* crime. Outside, she had again crossed the corner lot. This time, she had brushed her forehead against the thorn tree branch. The headbands she favored had not been style, but deceit. They hid a wound on that beautiful brow, a wound Leroy wouldn't have recalled from their escape.

Galway laid his hand on his partner's crooked back, walked with her toward her house. "Do you believe Johnny actually saw Beth?"

"I think he knew. He waited outside for her, but she didn't come. He could have stolen something specifically for her, something she asked for. Even if he didn't know then," Mrs. Dunbar continued, "he knew for sure after Earl Wellington visited him. She had been there."

"Earl knew it, too. She probably told him, at least enough."

"They both wanted to protect her."

"Good instincts, misused this time," Mrs. Dunbar said, with a husky voice Galway hadn't heard before.

"I'll call Andy," he said.

They were at the back steps. She tried to look up at him, but was too close and could only speak toward him. "Can't we do more than that? Right now? Can't we at least get Earl out of jail immediately? He didn't do *anything*."

Galway understood perfectly the impetus to right it all, and if not all, then at least one aspect. Save one person an injustice. "It's not that simple," he said. "We could make a legal misstep that might cause more harm than good." He thought about his invasion into Luke's house, the two journals he had returned with the others as though they had been in the group Andy obtained. "We may have already done so. Or I may have. Now that we have the information, it's best to let Andy use it. He's sharp about procedure. And actually, Mrs. Dunbar, Earl *did* do something. He knew the truth from the beginning. He lied. He impeded an investigation. He could easily be sentenced for his part alone, no matter his motives."

"That's absolutely disgusting. It's terrible." She took three of the remaining steps, and turned to look directly at him. "You can't let that happen, Galway. You know that would be terribly wrong, and you have a responsibility to keep it from happening."

"I do. I do have that responsibility. And that's why we shouldn't do anything more except call Andy. He's the expert. Trust me."

With a resigned sigh, she turned, grasped the screen door handle awkwardly, fumbled the door open and stepped into the small entry room off her kitchen. "Then call from here," she said, "so I can know help is on the way."

He sat down by the phone in her living room. As he dialed Andy's number, he was momentarily startled by what appeared to be a bird inside the house, on the window sill, but its very stillness revealed it as fake. Beautiful, but not real.

When he heard Andy's "Hello," Galway said, "I had it wrong, Buddy. Earl Wellington didn't kill Luke. Beth Wellington did."

Galway explained.

"I'm not surprised," Andy said. "This is like musical chairs for who did it. But it makes sense. Beth's story shifted around. She didn't offer any information until it was pretty evident you already knew it or soon would. She didn't mention the rug. Maybe she thought Leroy would incriminate himself if he mentioned it or even if he forgot it. We may find that second knife, trace it to her. You know, she may not even be pregnant. Have you thought of that?"

No. He hadn't. "I guess we'll know soon enough. Look, Andy, do you see any conflict if I represent Earl? I can withdraw from Johnny's case."

"We can work it out. I'll get started on it. What about the sister?"

Galway saw her fascinating eyes, the grace of her outward self.

"Maybe let the courts appoint someone. The man from Higginsville."

"Okay. Keep me closely posted. This is weaving like a Gordian knot."

Galway thought of Beth's mercurial nature. "I have to act pretty quickly. The sister may disappear entirely."

Standing at the sink, Mrs. Dunbar shook two aspirin from their bottle, filled a small paper cup with water, and swallowed the pills. She offered the bottle to Galway.

"Please," he said.

She took another small paper cup from the dispenser, filled it, and handed it to him.

"We should have eaten something first," she said.

"I'm not hungry."

"Neither am I." She opened a canister and offered him a cookie. "But that's not the point." When he took one, she took one herself.

Outside, walking slowly toward his house, he stopped part way. He didn't want to go home yet. He would like to skip ahead, pass up some of the emptiness. He had to call Bonnie. And in the near future he had to meet with both Walter and Bonnie, share a few details, make plans to talk the past year into their common history. The desire was there, but not the readiness. But soon. He'd take them out for a steak, or, better yet, join them for a day on a river bank and let them teach him how to fish. He wanted to thank the two of them for staying with him that terrible day last year, and that night, and the next day. Taking silent turns.

They had come together to his office. He knew when he saw them what it would be, though it couldn't be, nothing tragic in his life so suddenly. He didn't have anyone but his parents. His secretary had led them in, closed the door as she left. Bonnie said, "Galway, we have to tell you something hard, very hard." Walter came around the desk, leaned down a little, his hand on the arm of Galway's chair, and said softly, "It's your mom and dad."

They had driven him the forty miles to his parents' home, answering his few questions on the way. The neighbors had noticed no activity, no paper taken in. Apparently, when a cold spell hit, his parents' heater had automatically kicked on. They were in bed, at least that's how it appeared. They were asleep and never woke up. Carbon monoxide poisoning. So common an accident. So avoidable. So unbearably sad.

When he had emerged from the car, looking at his parents' home, it appeared already changed, as if it were blurred in memory. The white siding was soft and muted, the roof a dull, rippling red, as if the tiles had fused.

Inside, he knew his parents would not appear. The bodies had already been removed, taken for possible autopsies. And how could that be, to have parents gone and a past gone without a word or even a thought? He couldn't ask them one question.

Walter and Bonnie had let him roam through the rooms, though one would check on him in a few minutes, as if he were looking for a way out. He was looking for a note, an accidental note that gave him reason and solace. An object that had a symbolic interpretation he would immediately sense.

A house and things. No subtle word. No insight. Grief.

He had questions, and over the next few days he asked them. Had his parents been sleeping on their sides, his father's stomach to her back or the reverse? He didn't know why that mattered except he hadn't been able to see the farewell embrace. Had the alarm been set? For what time? He needed to check the clocks. He did so, too, eventually. The alarm wasn't set, but then what did that prove? His father always awakened early. The drapes were open, as if ready for the morning light.

They were too young to have planned to leave together like that. As far as he knew, neither was ill, or sad, or tired. They were vibrant, active people, needing nothing but each other. Absolutely nothing. Everything else was an afterthought, an addition, not the grand substance of their lives. Their wills were on file.

It was an accident. It was. They were over. He was here, having never won them.

17

Some People Love More Than Others

WEDNESDAY MORNING, GALWAY AND EARL WERE IN A PRIVATE, closed room, a deputy outside the door and a camera mounted in the corner, supposedly not recording sound, though Galway didn't trust that to be the case. He had drawn his chair closer to the corner of the square, unadorned table. He and Earl were facing each other, no hostility or wariness emanating from the young man. Instead, Galway noted a patient resignation in Earl that indicated the talk had no bearing on anything in his life. This was a sad and accepted end.

Not if Galway could help it.

"Earl," he said. "I want to make this simple for us both. No games. Just a straightforward explanation that answers the situation. Please tell me exactly how the death of Luke Michaels transpired. Tell me how and when you arrived at his house, what transpired between you, and when and how you left. That's it. From beginning to end."

"I believe I don't have to say anything. I confessed. That's enough."

"No, it's not. Many people confess to things they didn't do. For different reasons, of course, some admirable, some not."

"I prefer not to answer. I said what I had to say."

"You need to prove that you did it, if you don't want someone else to be considered."

"I think they'll be happy with me."

"Your attorney, if he's not worthless, won't let them be."

"And you're my attorney?"

"Yes."

"I choose to have another attorney. Nothing against you."

Galway nodded, leaned back. "Nothing against me except that I know you're lying." He matched Earl's silence for a while, wondered that the guy didn't just get up, knock on the door for the guard, and ask to go back to his cell. Maybe he didn't know he was allowed to do that. Maybe he was hoping for something to resolve the situation. Maybe he didn't give a damn what happened now. Was close to being dead.

Galway studied Earl's features—a good guy. Soft-hearted and in pain. "I know what it's like to love someone as you love Beth. It's an entire world separate from everything and everybody. It's not sexual. Don't get me wrong. It's just total. The laugh, the movements, the voice, the wonder of a complete joy, inexplicable. A closeness of unique kind and degree. The idea of it not being is terrifying—not to have it present anywhere in the world. You want to keep it perfect, guard it, give up whatever paltry thing you have or are to protect it. You allow no doubts about it. If they threaten, you seal them out because any imperfection is so slight it can't count. I know." Galway took a deep breath, closed his eyes a second, looked at Earl. "The feeling isn't ever going to leave you. It's not going to diminish. The pain you feel is possible only because of the love you feel. Some people love more than others. Maybe their love has some purpose other than to serve its object, maybe such love fuels the world, spills over to touch those who can't feel it themselves and never receive it. Loving like that is a great gift."

Earl's eyes were brimming but he didn't cry. He cleared his throat, coughed, smiled wanly at Galway, then gazed at the floor.

Silence fell around them, broken only faintly by a deep reverberation, like pressured doors not far away, a machine roaring on, massive trucks on a nearby highway. The world moving.

"I came in under the house," Earl began, "into the bedroom. Luke was sitting up, on the floor. I hadn't planned to hurt him, but to see how things were. She was worried sick. I needed to know how bad it was and what had to be done. He made a couple of remarks and I just let go. There was a knife in the floor and I grabbed it and swung it . . . right into his belly." He nodded curtly. "There. You have it."

"Where's the knife?"

"I don't remember when I dropped it. Maybe on the floor."

"Just one question. How did you leave the house?"

"Underneath, same as I came."

"Okay."

Galway stood up, patted Earl's shoulder. "You're a nice guy, too good for this kind of stuff."

"No," Earl said. "I'm not a nice guy."

"You can't make up for other people's weaknesses. There's not enough of you to live right for everyone."

"You have to take me at my word. I did what I said."

"No, you didn't."

She hadn't told him that she had scooted the dresser in place and had gone out the same window Johnny did. She had wanted Johnny to be blamed. Anyone but herself, including Earl.

* * *

Late Wednesday evening, the moon, exceedingly full and low, like a false dawn, washed the outside with a pearly glow. In one hand, Mrs. Dunbar carried an open can of paint, in the other, a paint brush. She worked around her own house first, applying a very thin blue line under each windowsill, where it would not be noticeable. From Galway's place came lilting music, sweet and pleasant. When she crossed to his house, her shadow preceded her, a sight that momentarily gave her pause, but she continued. This wasn't witchcraft. It wasn't even superstition. It was precaution. And it could, she reasoned, even be accepted as tradition. It was a little strip of faith and good wishes, a harmless gesture of safekeeping, a strip of blue to keep evil at bay. She did feel guilty. Holding the can steady, tiny as it was, took some effort, as did painting a short, straight line on the underside of his sills, too. She had a crooked body and the simplest things became more and more difficult. She suddenly wondered if, to an outsider, her shape and actions would look more than strange, like someone about a nefarious business. She was just an aging woman.

Galway listened to old albums that had belonged to his parents. Even the scratches and occasional skips were familiar to him. He didn't want to get off track, to forget who he was and the kind of life he wanted. To be a happy person, a good one. Beth Wellington was not what she had appeared to be. Or perhaps she was, and his vision had been temporarily weakened. He hoped the condition was temporary.

He had left the lamps off, and the moonlight fell into the room, outlining the heavy furniture, making pale paths of the little free space. A breeze crossed his shoulders and neck. He rose to look out the window at the peaceful night. He saw someone at the edge of his porch and went outside, barefooted, onto the damp grass. "Mrs. Dunbar," he said, into the darker area, where the moonlight didn't reach. "Mrs. Dunbar, what are you doing?"

He didn't really care what she answered. Here he was, at near midnight, with one adventure ended and another perhaps beginning. He still wasn't happy but he was happier. The woman had a gift.

~

Epilogue

GALWAY HADN'T PLANNED TO ATTEND LEROY AND ANNE'S wedding, but on the appointed afternoon, he drove through a hazy, fall day, with the breeze skittering stiff leaves across the walks and street, and parked at the curb opposite the church house. He admired the building. It was old, made of stone from the local quarry. The arched double-doors were black with age, heavy. High above them, centered beneath the steeple pitch, was a remarkably beautiful, round, stained-glass window. Through it, a muted light would soften the filled pews and touch the bride and groom like a blessing. He knew this because he had been inside the church just a few weeks ago, installing new, quiet, ceiling fans. While inside, he had examined the beautiful window, both how the glass sections joined, and how the entire piece was set into the wall. He might be called upon to install one someday. This was a first, personal lesson in a craftsmanship he would probably never attain. He had also sat atop his ladder and studied the empty room.

He was intrigued that Mrs. Dunbar was drawn to such a building and to services within it.

Now, the church doors opened and the wedding guests spilled out, flutters of colored silk over the lawn. They milled and laughed, watching the doors for the bride and groom. Among them were Earl and Johnny, standing side by side. Earl looked older, more somber, in a gray suit and white turtleneck. A lightness had been taken from his friendly face, but he still seemed solid, trustworthy. Beside him, Johnny was an aspiring something in sandals, no socks, dark cotton slacks, the latter hidden to mid-thigh by the tails of an absolutely white, oversized shirt. He stood with his hands down and clasped, as if he had to hold them still. He noticed the truck, smiled, and raised one hand in a brief half wave. He spoke to Earl, who looked at Galway and, after a few seconds, nodded stiffly.

Lives were changed.

The bride and groom came out. Leroy's strong-boned face bespoke pride and happiness. Next to him, Anne had been transformed from a handsome woman to a beautiful one. Her face was upturned repeatedly, toward Leroy. Good.

Rituals were necessary to make joy memorable. Otherwise, it was too fleeting.

He let the truck creep away.

In late afternoon, Galway walked over to Mrs. Dunbar's. She had upended two metal lawn chairs and was hosing them off.

"I would have helped," he said.

"I don't need help with this. Besides, I enjoy it."

She obviously did. Her slacks and tennis shoes were mud-splattered.

"I guess the wedding was well attended," Galway said.

"Very. And the music was wonderful. Earl Wellington sang."

"I wish I'd heard that."

"You *could* have. I expected you to show up at the last minute. I even saved a seat for you."

"I thought about it. But I didn't want to be in any of the photos. It was their day. Their memory."

Her appraising expression turned to one of fondness. "I see." She tossed the hose aside. The hose snaked toward her empty flower bed, water gushing across the loosened soil. "Darn," she said.

Galway headed for the spigot. "I'll get it." He turned the water off, rolled up the hose and placed it on the flat rock under the spigot, as he had seen her do. Then he joined her on the steps.

"Are you busy tomorrow afternoon?" she asked.

"I don't have to be. I can move my jobs around. Why?"

"I want to go to the Musicians' Arte and I'm not confident about driving in that part of town."

"May I ask why you're going there?" He suspected he knew, but he wanted to let her play it out, as they did for one another.

"Johnny works there, from one to five." With a satisfied smile and an unusual lightness to her step, she took old towels from a box on the porch and tossed one to him.

"We have to get the chairs really dry or they'll rust," she said.

"Not if they're painted."

"You can't paint inside the cracks, or around the screws."

"You can't get towels in there either."

"It's the best we can do, unless you have a hair dryer."

He shook his head. "So Johnny's working in the music store? We couldn't have planned that better."

"He showed me a disassembled harmonica. He's doing something with the reeds."

"It's almost a happy ending," Galway said.

"All some people need is a little nudge in the right direction at the right time."

She dragged one chair out into the fading sun and he followed her with the other. They smiled and looked around their neighborhood. It had changed so quickly from the lush green and heavy scents of summer. Now came the lower sky, the sudden, golden sunsets, the silence of empty streets, and the lure of warm hearths and companionship.

ABOUT THE AUTHOR

B.A.L. McMillan is a Missouri writer originally from Gravel Hill, Missouri. She is a student of psychology, herbal medicine, folk lore, religion, animals, and of literature on the subjects of ghosts, witches, and angels. She writes traditional mysteries and fantasies.